A ROBOT GIRL RUINED my SLEEPOVER

WRITTEN and illustrated by
REBECCA PATTERSON

ANDERSEN PRESS

First published in 2020 by
Andersen Press Limited
20 Vauxhall Bridge Road
London SW1V 2SA
www.andersenpress.co.uk

2 4 6 8 10 9 7 5 3 1

British Library Cataloguing in Publication Data available.

ISBN 978 1 78344 947 7

Printed and bound in Great Britain by
Clays Limited, Elcograf S.p.A.

For Susanna

CHAPTER ONE

'HURRY UP, GUS!' I yelled from the car, 'I do NOT want to be late!'

My little brother Gus had spent the last five minutes rolling about on the launch pad having a massive strop about not being allowed to take Sparks, our cyborg cat, in for Show and Tell.

'Whyyy not?' he was yelling, 'I don't see whyyyyy NOT!'

'Because he's worth a fortune and he's not a toy!' said Mum, getting into the car.

Gus stopped rolling, but he was still just lying there, looking up at all the cars in the sky.

'I'm counting to three and then I'm flying off!' said

Mum, firing up the jets. Gus turned his head to look at us and scratched his ear.

I sighed and folded my arms and said to no one, 'I cannot tell you how much I'd prefer a big sister called Tamara!'

Mum started counting, 'One . . . two . . .' and placed her finger dramatically over the lift-off button. Gus got to his feet, dragged his bag across the floor and clambered in next to me, 'Shove up, Boggle McScruff Pants!!' he said.

'Gus!' said Mum, smiling a little as she flew up to join the other cars in the Fly Zone.

Gus admired the reflection of his chubby face in the curved glass of the windows, 'Your best friend Bianca said I'm the cutest kid in Year One!'

I ignored him and carried on looking out of the window, down at the buildings and trees.

Gus carried on, 'Eight and a half people in my class want to marry me already! No one wants to marry you, Lyla!' he said, prodding me.

'Good, 'cause I don't want to get married!' I snapped back.

'How can half a person want to marry you?' laughed Mum, as we landed on the Lime Grove Edu Hub launch pad.

'Evan is the half because he's in love with me and Laura!' explained Gus breezily, as he jumped out. Mum did her *Isn't-he-just-adorable* face at me.

· ☀·⭐·☀ *

I ran down the launch-pad steps. In the distance my best friend Bianca waved. She ran towards me as I charged across the playground, 'Hi, Lyla!' she yelled.

'Hi! Hey, I made you this,' I said, 'at the weekend.'

I gave Bianca the tiny model of her I'd made out of my Clay 'n' Move set. I'm quite good at making models and this stuff is good, once the model is dried it can shuffle about a few steps by itself. She looked at the little figure walking about in her palm, 'Aww, it's cute!' she laughed. 'But I'm not that lumpy! How big did you make my ears?! And look at my nose!'

'Oh it's pretty accurate!' I laughed and ran on towards the portals.

Bianca chased behind me laughing, saying she'd do one of me and include my big bug eyes.

We sat down on the wall giggling and calling each other Bug Eyes and Lumpy in stupid voices.

Mercedes turned to us, 'Gonna be interesting today!'

'What is?' I said

'The visitors!'

I looked puzzled.

Mercedes stood in front of me, hands on hips, 'Duh! Lyla! How can you forget? I know you're a bit slow but Mr Caldwell's only been going on about this for like ever!'

'I'm not slow!' I said.

Mercedes shrugged, 'OK, well you're not slow . . . dreamy?'

'Dreamy?'

'I mean you spend a lot of time in class drawing on your hands,' said Mercedes, looking down at all the little white flowers and stars I'd doodled on the back of my fingers and hadn't washed off.

Bianca showed Mercedes the little clay figure I'd made, 'But look what she did for me! It's a tiny me in clay! It can walk!'

Mercedes didn't look too impressed, 'Girlfriend, Clay 'n' Move is for little kids!'

I looked up and across the playground and saw two boys from our class, James and Burak, strutting about with their arms straight out in front. They were putting on silly robot voices, 'I AM A BA-BY RO-BOT! BEEP! BEEP! I WILL DO YOUR MATHS? ALLOW ME TO DO YOUR SPEL-LING TEST!'

And then I remembered, 'Oh yeah! The cyborg robot kids come today!'

The two boys came over. James pushed his cool moonshades up his nose, 'Robot day is here! This is gonna be so funny!'

'I know! Maybe we'll have to get them out of their boxes when they arrive,' said Mercedes, 'like massive dolls!'

Burak shook his head, 'Nah, I've seen the adverts for these. They look good, realistic. Way better than Old Junky Smelly!' He nodded towards the other side of the playground where Mr Martinelli, our ancient electronic school caretaker, was telling Louis MacAvoy to land his flyke, his metallic-sounding voice barking, **'STOP LOOP THE LOOPS AND LAND. REPEAT. STOP LOOP THE LOOPS!'**

'Mr Martinelli is so old!' said Bianca. 'Look how he rolls now!'

Mr Martinelli is really just a big metal bucket thing with a few lights. Everyone calls him Mr Junky Smelly. You can say it to his face because he is such a primitive robot with really basic hearing and he can't tell the difference. We used to have an electronic playground assistant called Miss Fritz, but she got upgraded with a new motherboard and was so much better at everything that she left our school last December and became an estate agent on Mars.

Louis landed his flyke, 'There you go, Mr Junky Smelly! I'm down on the ground.'

Mr Martinelli flashed a green light, which is his low energy way of saying 'OK', and rolled away.

'Hope these electric kids are better than that old can!' laughed James.

Louis sat down next to us on the little wall and put on a serious face, 'Yeah, but the trouble is, these latest electric kids — they're not safe! That's what my uncle Dan says, lots of glitches. I'm keeping well away from them! Well away!'

James nudged him and said, 'Louis you're not going to be allowed near one, mate!'

'What do you mean?'

'Come on, Louis, you're not exactly reliable. Who tried to set fire to the school skybus?'

'When I was seven!' said Louis, folding his arms. 'That's ages ago!'

It's true, Louis MacAvoy is officially the naughtiest boy in our class, and in the last few weeks he's been even worse, but he's actually quite nice. He's as short as me. Maybe even shorter. At break he hangs out in the little kids' playground showing off to them. I've heard him tell them his real dad is a trillionaire and has a Chrysler Comet Intergalactic with a gold tint windscreen. He sits next to me now in class. I used to sit next to Bianca but two weeks ago Louis was messing about so much at the back on his floaty seat going, 'I'm Mr Wobble! All hail The Wobbleman!!' Mr Caldwell told him to swap places with Bianca at the front.

· ✳·⭐·✳ *

Bianca put the little clay model away in her pocket. 'Thanks for this, Lyla. It is really sweet,' she said quietly. Then Mr Caldwell opened the classroom portal and we all went in. The boys shoved their coats into the suction hatches discussing all the terrible ways an electric child could kill you. Louis had heard they can pass on a strange electrical disease that makes your own eyes glow like car headlights for the rest of your life. Felicity rolled her eyes and said to Franka and Mercedes, 'They're totally safe. I'm just worried they're gonna be really super pretty! The ones I saw on the adverts are like models!'

'But you ARE really pretty!' squealed Franka.

Felicity shrugged, 'Yeah, I guess we're all quite attractive in this class in our own different ways.'

'Yeah!' agreed Amia, tossing her hair. 'And the people who aren't so super pretty make up for it by having . . . great . . .' she paused and glanced at me, 'personalities!'

Bianca nudged me, 'That's right, Bug Eyes. You have a great personality!'

'Just like you, Lumpy,' I laughed back.

· ✳ ⋆ ✳ ·

I walked into the classroom and sat next to Louis.

'Oi, keep your elbows on your side of the desk, Pie Face!' said Louis, helping himself to my stylus, my memory cube and two of my highglowers.

I wouldn't mind him borrowing my stuff if he didn't give it back to me half chewed and all spitty!

Mr Caldwell said we had just a few minutes before our amazing visitors arrived, 'This is a first!' he said excitedly. 'Cyborg children about to take part in mainstream education alongside normal organic ones like you lot. You can tell your grandkids you were part of history!'

'Yeah, well, my uncle Dan says they're not safe,' said Louis.

'Yeah,' said Mercedes, 'what if they go rogue and try to kill us?!'

Mr Caldwell tutted and rolled his eyes to the ceiling, 'Nonsense, the Luna Livewires Corporation has been perfecting these children for years . . . And here they are now!'

CHAPTER TWO

A very elegant woman came into our classroom with really smooth skin and glossy hair. She had a smart little sash across her suit which said, 'LUNA LIVEWIRES CORPORATION – Building better children for a better universe!' She gave a little wave back to whoever was still out in the corridor and said softly, 'Just wait outside for now,' then she turned to face us. 'Hello, children. My name is Sophia System 4002 and I'm from the Luna Livewires Corporation based on the Cassini Crater region of the Moon where we create real cyborg children! Some of you may be surprised to learn that I am a cyborg myself!'

Everyone made 'Wow!' faces at each other and

Louis whispered to me, 'Better than old rust bucket Junky Smelly. No visible wires. She's a babe!'

Sophia System 4002 went on, 'Well, if you think I'm impressive for a cyborg, wait till you see our new range of children cyborgs. They're wonderful! So totally human that the government has decided that soon they will be allowed to enter normal, mainstream Edu Hubs, just like yours.'

Louis muttered in my ear, 'Here we go, more Battery Brains driving us all crazy. Like we need any more robots.'

Sophia System 4002 heard. She looked straight at Louis with such a focused stare that Louis slid down a little in his chair, 'Young man, I can assure you the children you are about to meet can be every bit as human, thoughtful, and charming as you are if . . .' she tilted her head on one side and looked super caring, '. . . they are loved.'

'Oh my darling!' said James, kissing his memory cube. Which got big laughs and Mr Caldwell stomped to the back of the class to have a little word with him. Sophia raised one perfectly arched eyebrow and went on, 'You are all used to your cyborg pets at home and your wonderful electronic school assistants. But this is where our cyborg children differ, they actually grow more human the more you care for them. Show them kindness and love and they will thrive. We can't program friendship up on the Moon in our factory, but here they can meet all of you and learn friendship from your kind, caring ways.'

'Caring ways? Has she been to our school?!' said Mercedes, shaking her head.

'Well, I think you all look very caring.' Sophia smiled and went on, 'Now, what I want you to do is think about which three children in this class would make the best volunteers? I need three of you to look after my cyborg children during the days when we visit your school. I'm looking for kind, committed children who can help our young cyborgs. They don't need help with things like maths or spelling, but they do need kindness.

We will be coming into your Edu Hub every Monday, Wednesday and Friday this term. Remember a lot of things will seem strange to them, they've had a very protected life so far. I need the most reliable, gentle and helpful students in this class to work with these children.'

Mr Caldwell walked to the front and said, 'Thanks, Sophia, I know we're all really excited about this. We've got some super responsible children here in Year Six so hands up who would like to look after a cyborg child!'

Everyone stuck their hands up.

Everyone! Burak was doing that lifting his bottom off his seat thing so his hand was higher and saying, 'Please, Mr C! Me! Pick meee!' Franka and Felicity were getting one arm to hold the other hand up, like that makes their hand go up higher!

And loads of people were making straining noises, like holding your arm up is as hard as weight lifting.

'Well, I'm not picking any silly people who behave like they're still in Reception! Lyla, how about you?'

'Yes, Mr Caldwell,' I said, 'I'd love to!'

I heard Felicity whisper to someone, 'Lyla? She draws on her hands!'

But I didn't care! I was suddenly excited and nervous like you feel before you have to present your project to the class.

Mr Caldwell did his slow scanning round the class at all the straining arms, 'James Defries, apart from your silly shouting out earlier I think you'd actually make quite a good mentor and now I need . . . one more . . .'

His eyes stopped at Louis who was, for once, sitting very quietly with his hand in the air like a model pupil.

'Louis, really? You've been making some bad choices lately. Getting a bit silly. Do you really think you'd be a good mentor?'

'Yes, sir! I would,' Louis folded his arms across his chest and looked back at the class, 'I can be OK . . . if I want to.' Then he put his head down onto his folded arms and looked a little defeated, 'Plus I need something . . . better in my life right now. I'm having problems with . . .' His voice trailed away to a sigh. Sophia System 4002 turned towards Mr Caldwell and said really quietly, so only the people right at the front like me could hear, 'I sense sadness, why don't we give him a chance?'

'OK, Louis! You're our final volunteer!' said Mr Caldwell.

Burak muttered, 'Not fair!'

Louis went, 'Yess!' punched the air with his fist and shoved me lightly, 'Hey, Pie Face, we both got a cyborg!!'

'You said you wouldn't go near one 'cause of electrical diseases,' I whispered.

'Changed my mind,' shrugged Louis, 'These sound cool. They're from the Moon, gonna be high-spec.'

Then I whispered even more quietly, 'Are you sad?'

'Not now, I'm not!' Louis said, sitting up extra straight, looking all excited.

Sophia System 4002 smiled very brightly, 'Right, let's bring in our new friends!'

A beautifully dressed girl walked in. She looked like an eleven-year-old girl only . . . better. Everything about her shimmered, her flawless skin, her glittery hair, her perfect shoes. The whole class went 'Aaaah!' softly like they'd just seen a firework. She stood there blinking her big eyes slowly and looking about at all of us.

'Hello, everyone! My name is Clara 2.2.'

Her voice wasn't anything like Mr Martinelli's robotty one. It was a calm, gentle voice. She didn't look nervous like I do when I have to stand up and talk in front of everyone. She didn't go, 'Um . . . er . . .' and she didn't go bright red and look down at her shoes. She just stood at the front looking all clean and said, 'I'm a second generation Clara, the first Claras were very good at maths but I am very good at maths and sport. I speak every Earth language and have two Moon dialects. I believe that friendship is the most valuable currency in the universe!'

Felicity and Franka said, 'Ahh, so true!'

I heard Burak whisper to Mercedes, very quietly, 'Yuck. I'm going to be sick.'

It was way too quiet for Mr Caldwell, but Clara 2.2 turned her perfect head towards Burak and said, 'Are you unwell? May I assist you?'

Burak looked embarrassed, 'Um, no, I suddenly feel a bit better now, thanks!'

Clara 2.2 smiled at him, 'Oh good!

You organic children feel sick sometimes but cyborg children are never ill, we are here to understand your pain and help you. I am designed to bring you joy and laughter every day!'

'Better if she brought us no maths tests and a five-day weekend!' laughed Louis.

'LOUIS!' said Mr Caldwell.

Sophia System 4002 frowned at Louis and then called in the next cyborg, a boy with very neat black hair and a cheeky smile. He looked even more confident than Clara 2.2 and said, 'Hi, guys! I'm Felix Tranquility X. I'm currently eleven point five years old and what is known as a peacekeeper. I'm diplomatic, calm and have been designed to be charming at all times. I am fully proficient in all subjects. I am what is known as a Universal Friend Model, meaning I can make friends with anybody!'

'Oh yeah! Try me,' said Louis under his breath, 'I'm the Universal Annoy Everyone Model.'

I smiled at him and whispered, 'Only some of the time.'

But he's right, he does do some stupid stuff, he's been even more of an idiot this term wobbling about being Mr Wobbleman and he doesn't really have a best friend. Felix Tranquility X looked straight at Louis from under his perfect eyebrows and said, 'Just looking at you, human boy, I feel we have been friends forever. I feel we have shared secrets and played games in golden sun.'

Louis just rolled his eyes and looked out of the window so Mr Caldwell came right over to his desk and hissed, 'Louis, you have been given the opportunity to look after one of our cyborg friends today, but from the way you are currently behaving I am having doubts about letting you. Do I make myself quite clear?'

Louis nodded. Felix Tranquility X gave me a little friendly wink, but maybe it was just an electrical fault, anyway, I winked back. I was so excited – these children looked amazing! Especially compared to people like Louis!

Then the last cyborg entered the classroom.

Except we didn't see him come in, we saw the door open but not him, because he was shorter than the desks! Sophia System 4002 picked him up so he could stand on the front desk while he introduced himself.

He looked like a boy of about eleven but he was just very small. Felicity and some other girls went, 'Aaah, adorable!' and, 'Sooo cute!' but the little cyborg boy looked really cross and said, 'Excuse me! I am actually eleven! And I have a genius level IQ! I am proficient in all medicine and astrophysics and my name is Jasper Microrange Express. Yes, I am a compact product, but I am the future! In an overcrowded universe I function at a high level while taking up much less space. I also require fewer materials to produce. I am the way forward!'

'Wow!' said Louis, and then turned to me, 'I told you they'd be good. My real dad says stuff from the Moon Colonies is always top quality. That thing's amazing!'

'Thanks for your support,' said Jasper Microrange Express.

Louis shot his hand up, 'Mr Caldwell, can I be partners with that one, the little one!'

'Oh, all right, Louis can be with Jasper, and James you can be with Felix, and Lyla's with Clara 2.2.'

Clara 2.2 gave me this really friendly smile and did a tiny wave.

Mr Caldwell went on, 'They are to stay with you all day, every Monday, Wednesday and Friday, attend all lessons with you and understand what being at a normal Edu Hub with human children is like. Remember they are here to learn friendship so let's show them just how friendly we are at Lime Grove. If they get on well we might allow them to go to your homes for playdates at a later stage, to fully integrate them into our human world!'

Apart from Mercedes folding her arms across her chest and rolling her eyes at Mr Caldwell's babyish use of the word 'playdate', everyone else started chatting excitedly.

Amia shouted, 'Mr C, can we take them swimming? Can they go in the Aquadome? Or will they like fuse or something?'

'What do they eat?' said Felicity. 'Are they gluten free? Vegan? Will we get the correct information concerning the cyborg diet?!'

Ridwan wanted to know if he might have an allergic reaction to cyborgs as he was pretty sensitive to some polymers and plastics and his mum might not be too keen to have one in the house.

Mr Caldwell waved his hands and said, 'OK! OK! Let's all calm down. Enough questions for now. I'm sure our new friends will be happy to explain all there is to know about being a cyborg child soon enough. Ah, look it's almost break. Outside everyone! Take your cyborgs!'

CHAPTER THREE

I walked up to my Clara 2.2 and she shook my hand, hers was smooth and cool.

'Oh Lyla! I was so pleased when you got me. I just knew in my heart we'd be great friends!'

'Oh me too!' I said, 'Come on, let's go outside. I love your dress!'

Bianca caught up with us in the coatpod, 'Hey, Lyla, I'll help you with yours, yeah?'

'OK!' I said, going out of the portal to the playground, holding my cyborg's hand for her safety.

Clara 2.2 turned back and said softly to Bianca, 'I don't need help because I am perfect!'

Bianca said, 'Plastic fantastic!' under her breath.

Clara 2.2 turned round again, but this time super fast, and said, 'Bianca don't be so silly! I am fantastic but I am not plastic, I am collagen.'

· ✳·⭐.✳ *

The second we got out into the playground everyone huddled around us. It was crazy! All the girls were inspecting Clara's hair and saying stuff like, 'Can you use conditioner on it? Is it nylon?' Amia was lifting up Clara's skirt! To see if her legs were normal or had hinges and even poked about in her hair looking for solar cells.

I took charge, 'Don't crowd her! I'm in charge of this one. Stand back! Back!'

Everyone moved back, I can be quite authoritative when I have to.

I held tight onto Clara 2.2's hand, 'OK all you lot can ask questions one at a time — like a press conference thing. I'm going to stand up on the wall with my Clara and the rest of you can ask questions! ONE AT A TIME!' I repeated firmly.

'Yes, sir!' laughed Bianca and saluted me like a soldier, and I would have laughed but I was actually a bit stressed.

I got up on the wall and Clara 2.2 jumped up next to me in one smooth slow motion.

The crowd of nosey kids surged even closer to the wall, staring at us.

A snotty Year Three girl poked my leg and said, 'How come you get to keep her?'

'I'm not keeping her, I'm the responsible Year Six person looking after her. OK, let's have some questions for our beautiful cyborg friend!' I said above the sea of amazed faces looking up at us, 'You! Year Two girl, at the back, a question for our cyborg visitors? Sorry, don't know your name.'

The small Year Two girl said, 'Does your hair grow?'

'Hello, Dono Yername!' said Clara 2.2, 'Our hair grows and we grow all over just like you! We're programmed to grow up into perfectly wonderful adults and then just stay like that, fully functioning, young-ish adults!'

'Do you die?' shouted out Burak from the back.

'I'm fully guaranteed for one hundred years!' said Clara 2.2. 'And I'm completely recyclable!' she said, patting her hair, and sounding just a little smug.

From our higher up position on the little wall I could see across the playground to the far side, near the real bushes, where Louis was strutting about with Jasper Microrange Express. He had tied one of the skipping ropes round Jasper's little waist and was leading him about like a dog. 'Come on, Jaspy! Come on! There's a good little cyby!'

Mercedes turned round and looked across the playground, shielding her eyes from the morning sun, 'Why did they let him have one? Me and Amia would have been waaaay more responsible!'

Then Mr Martinelli wobbled over to Louis and we saw

him tell him off in his slow voice and Louis answering back, 'But, Mr Junky Smelly, he likes it! He's not bothered. I have to be RESPONSIBLE! Don't want him running off like a lost dog, do I?! He's worth millions!'

Now most of our press conference were looking over, 'He'll break that poor little thing!' said Franka.

'And he's so . . . insensitive. Treating him like a puppy!' muttered Felicity.

'Mr Caldwell wants his brain testing for letting Louis anywhere near that little cyborg! Louis is such an idiot,' said Amia.

Clara 2.2 put her arm round my shoulder and said to the crowd, 'But I am so lucky! I have the amazing Lyla Hastings looking after me! Lyla is so clever and sensible! I'm sure she has many admirers in this school.'

Bianca sniggered.

And just then Gus barged to the front of the crowd and yelled, 'NO! NO! SHE DOES NOT! NOT AS MANY AS ME. EIGHT AND A HALF PEOPLE WANT TO MARRY ME!'

'Shh, Gus!' I said and then turned to Clara 2.2, 'It's my brother.'

Gus wouldn't shut up!

'HEY, ELECTRIC GIRL! DO YOU POO? I BET YOU POO . . . BATTERIES!'

The whole crowd laughed, even Bianca!

'Enough, Gus!' I said above the noise.

But no one was listening to me or even looking at Clara 2.2! My stupid little brother was running about in a small circle making farty noises and going, 'I poop batteries! I POOP BATTERIES!'

I tried to say, 'Any further questions for my cyborg friend before the end of break?' But half the crowd had walked away laughing and the smaller ones were off chasing about with Gus yelling, 'I POOP BATTERIES! I POOP BATTERIES!'

Mr Martinelli began to circle the playground, his croaky robot voice turned up to maximum, 'ALERT! BREAK OVER ALERT!' It was time to go back in.

Clara 2.2 walked ahead of us all, strutting back into the classroom quickly, 'More fun and learning. Come on, Lyla! Let's hurry back inside.'

As Bianca and I shoved our coats into the suction hatches, James walked past with his cyborg following close behind. James mouthed, 'Mine's SO BORING!' at us. Bianca smiled at him.

'James!' I whispered, 'Don't, I bet they lip read really well! Don't hurt their feelings!'

'They're just tech,' he laughed back, 'they don't have feelings.'

'Yes they do, Sophia said they have to learn friendship, they're really advanced!' I whispered back. 'And mine's really nice!'

'Well . . . for a suck-up!' said Bianca, walking into the classroom.

Mr Caldwell let Clara 2.2 and Felix Tranquility X sit up at the front of the classroom. Louis had put Jasper Microrange Express on his desk like a mascot and was stroking his little head.

'He's not a pet!' I whispered.

'He's better than yours!' he hissed back. 'Anyway, it relaxes him.'

Mr Caldwell said it was history and we had to do more on our projects. He turned to Felix Tranquility X, 'So, Felix, do you know much history?'

'What is it you need to know, sir?' smiled Felix

Tranquility X. 'Although I am not created for education excellence I might have the answer you require.'

'Could you tell the class something about our topic, the First Moon Settlers?'

'Certainly, sir! In what language?'

Mr Caldwell's eyes widened, 'Oh, well . . . English for now!'

Felix Tranquility X closed his eyes slowly and tilted his head back, 'Just recovering data, sir.'

'Ha! He's buffering!' shouted Louis.

'Louis!' said Mr Caldwell.

Felix began, 'The First Settlers arrived on the Moon in March 2071, although there had been several more primitive expeditions in the twentieth and twenty-first centuries . . .'

And he went on.

And on.

And in the end Mr Caldwell had to tap him on his shoulder and say, 'That's impressive but it has been forty minutes!'

· ✳·⭐·✳ ·

At lunch time I took Clara 2.2 to the lunch pod, Bianca came with us, reluctantly. 'Maybe Clara would like to mix with other pupils at lunch,' she said.

'But, Bianca, I'm in charge of Clara. I can't leave her wandering about by herself at lunch time! Look at the lunch pod, how would Clara cope in here without me?'

The lunch pod is crazy! Full of yelling kids and dinnerbots beeping and trying to suck up all the dropped peas and wipe the tables with their spindly metal arms. Everyone is shoving in the food queue and more dinnerbots are trying to keep us all in order droning on and on, 'NO PUSHING! NO PUSHING!' and making the little lights flash on top of their heads. The food choices clatter out of the old food hatches because Mr Martinelli never oils them. Clara placed her hands over her ears and said softly, 'Minimise volume input.' She flicked her earlobes with her smooth fingers and turned to me, her big eyes blinking and smiled, 'That's better. Quieter. You should do yours.'

'I wish I could!' I shouted above the din.

I got my usual two pots of pasta, Bianca got her vegan seaweed thing. As we walked through the beeping dinnerbots and found a place to sit I asked Clara 2.2 why she hadn't got any lunch. She giggled, 'I don't eat lunch! I don't have to. I make energy through my lustrous, smooth skin, I'm photovoltaic!'

Then she did a little twirl before she sat down and said, '"Clara 2.2 turning light into brilliance!" That's what it says in my adverts.'

I said, 'My adverts say "Lyla Basic Model turning pasta into just average"!'

Bianca laughed, but Clara 2.2 said, 'Is there an advert for you?'

'Um. No,' I said, chewing some of the pasta.

Clara placed her hand on my wrist, 'Well, I think there should be an advert for you! You're amazing!'

Bianca laughed so hard her Luna Lime juice came out of her nose which made her laugh even more.

Clara looked puzzled then said, 'Oh yes! Let's laugh! We are having so much fun! Ha ha ha! HA HA HA!'

Her laugh was strange, like the sound of bubbling water, and the children near us stopped eating and turned to stare. Then Clara stopped laughing as suddenly as she had started and said, 'What wonderful funny girls! But I like you best Lyla because your nose doesn't leak.'

This made Bianca giggle all over again.

Just then Louis walked behind our seats, Jasper Microrange Express walked in front of him carrying Louis' food on a tray. 'Got mine doing a few jobs already!' he said proudly. 'Training him up! Shove in, Pie Face! Let the little lad get through.'

I moved my chair in to let tiny Jasper walk past.

Clara 2.2 opened her big eyes even wider and looked really shocked, 'Why does he call you . . . Pie . . . Face?!'

I shrugged as I stood up to clear my stuff, 'He does it all the time, suppose he thinks my face looks sort of round like a pie?'

'But her very dear closest friends call her Bug Eyes,' said Bianca, still trying not to giggle again as she cleared her stuff and walked off to the degraders.

Clara looked shocked. She got up and walked really close to me as I went to the degraders, 'Pie Face? Bug Eyes? But you are the most beautiful girl in the class!'

I stopped and looked at her, 'Really?'

Clara nodded like she meant it and said softly, 'Inside and out.'

I walked with a little more sass to catch up with Bianca by the degraders.

'Why do you have to be so silly round Clara?' I whispered, scraping my leftover stuff off my plate.

Bianca shrugged, 'Because everything it says is so dumb and creepy!'

'She's not an "IT"! She's almost human! She just needs care and attention.'

Bianca groaned, 'Lyla! You'll be making friends with a calculator next!'

CHAPTER FOUR

I didn't say much to Bianca after lunch. We all sat on the little wall, Clara 2.2 between us, looking at the children rushing about. Louis ran up to us excited, 'Look at you lot like old ladies sitting about. Mine's so much more fun! Jasper's brilliant! Watch what my little lad can do with a football. Go on, Jasper! Show Pie Face, Clarabot and Bianca.'

He threw a football to Jasper who kicked it hard. The ball shot into the sky. But it didn't come down it just went on going! Straight up! Through the clouds! Louis folded his arms like a proud dad, 'We won't be seeing that again, my little friend here can get stuff into the stratosphere!'

'How many footballs have you got him to kick into space?!' I asked.

'Only four,' said Jasper, he tilted his tiny head on one side rather sweetly, 'but I can do more if you'd like?'

'Probably that's enough,' I smiled back. 'Here comes Mr C!'

'LOUIS! What's this I've just heard?!' Mr Caldwell said as he stormed out of the portal, 'About kicking footballs into space?'

Louis looked at him with his arms folded, 'Aaw! Who told on me this time? Bet it was Felicity or Burak.'

'Never mind that! What on earth are you doing with Jasper Microrange?'

'Mr Caldwell, these are good, obedient cyborgs,' said Louis and he shrugged like it was all beyond his control. 'Their instinct is to follow orders!'

'Shame the orders being given are TOTALLY RIDICULOUS, LOUIS! That's two extra lunch times in for you!'

Louis looked at the floor and Jasper put his tiny hand up to hold onto one of Louis' fingers.

Mr Caldwell spoke more calmly, 'You have been entrusted with a very valuable piece of technology, it's a real chance to show how responsible you can be. Don't make me regret my decision. Understand?'

Louis nodded.

· ✳ ⭐ ✳ ·

In the afternoon it was a maths test, Clara said to Mr Caldwell, 'I sense that my best friend Lyla needs my help with this test, sir.' But Mr Caldwell said the three cyborg children had to sit to one side.

Sophia System 4002 came back into our classroom to collect the three cyborgs near the end of the day. They had to fly back to their storage facility in the Luna Livewires Corporation factory. 'We will be back on Wednesday for more fun and learning!' she said as they all walked out in a neat line, their steps in time like small soldiers, and boarded their skyvan up on the launch pad.

Louis ran to the classroom window and pressed his face up to it so he could watch their skyvan disappear through the clouds, but Mr Caldwell said he had to sit back down as he'd only done two questions so far and if he didn't do more before the end of the day he'd be in at break tomorrow.

On the back of the skyvan was a little label saying Replica Humans on Board.

Gus was jealous about us having the cyborgs in our class. He was so mad he leaned forward in his seat in the car on the way home to complain to Mum, 'But why didn't we get any in Year One? Why?'

Mum was stressed about getting in the right lane up in the skyway, 'Shh Gus!' she said, 'back in your seat! I can't see what's flying over us!'

Gus sank back into his seat, 'S'not fair! Why don't they visit us in Year One? We're way more fun!'

45

'You'd break them,' I said. 'Plus you ask them stupid questions about how they poo!'

'Oh yes!' said Gus, 'That was funny!

'Clara didn't think so,' I said.

'But all the REAL children did!' laughed Gus, 'I POOP BATTERIES!' And he laughed so hard he had to support himself on the armrest.

Our car flew over the Trading Hub Dome and then over the central district, towards our neighbourhood with all the houses with their flat launch pads and long straight groves of trees in between. 'I feel sorry for the cyborg kids, made in a factory,' I said, 'I don't think they've ever been out anywhere before. It's sad for them.'

'I don't care!' said Gus, jumping out of the car as we landed on our launch pad, 'I was made in Mum and I've been to Florida!' He dropped his coat, his Edu Hub bag and his shoes all over the hall as he dashed inside.

'I bet cyborg kids don't just dump their stuff!' said Mum.

And Gus muttered, 'I'm not programmed for tidiness!' as Mum made him pick it all up.

In the kitchen I poured some Luna Lime. 'Hi, Dad,' I said and picked up Sparks, our little cyborg cat and put him on my shoulder. I carried on talking about the cyborgs, 'Clara 2.2 is really nice and she likes me loads already. She has this really shiny dress, she's sort of super girly but cool, if that makes sense? They're all really clever, they know everything! Felix knew masses of history just off the top of his head!'

'Boring snoring!' said Gus. 'Can they take themselves apart in little bits and hold their own head in their hands?'

'I don't think so.'

'Can they fly?'

'I didn't ask.'

'Can they make a laser beam come out of their eyes and burn through walls?'

'I hope not!' said Dad, who was tinkering about inside our broken teleporter. 'You wouldn't want that sort of thing happening in Lime Grove Edu Hub!'

'I would!' said Gus. 'Is the teleporter still broken?'

'Yeah,' said Dad. 'Keeps sending the fruit through too big! Look at the bananas!'

'Cool!' said Gus. 'Can I eat one?'

Dad nodded and carried on twiddling the knobs inside the teleporter. Gus peeled the banana and placed the big yellow banana skin on his head, arranging it like a sort of yellow pointy hat with long flaps down to his elbows.

'You better eat all that, Gus!' said Dad, but Gus wandered off to look at himself in the hall mirror.

'Do I look like a mermaid or an octopus?'

I didn't answer, I just went on, 'Anyway, Mr Caldwell said we might be able to have them home for visits, so they get to know all about human society! If we can take them home, Dad, can Clara come for a sleepover? That would be good for her friendship skills and independence and stuff.'

'We'll have to see, these very new cyborgs are worth a fortune! Sounds like a big ask having one actually in your house with no real training.'

'But they're not difficult to look after, Dad! They're not all clunky like the old Edu Hub robots. They don't spark or buzz. They're just perfect children!'

'Like me then!' said Gus, wandering back and tossing a banana peel flap over his shoulder like hair.

I walked off to my room. In the hall I gave a little look at my reflection, 'Plus, my Clara said I was the most beautiful girl in the class!' I shouted back to Gus.

'Yeah right!' said Gus. 'She sees you as fuzzy pixels, Lyla! You probably look OK pixelated!'

· ✳·⭐·✳ ·

I was almost too excited to sleep that Monday night. Having Clara at school was like having a present, the most amazing new toy even though I knew she wasn't mine to keep. Actually on Tuesday, when the cyborgs weren't in school, I couldn't shut up about them! 'I love how they're so . . . perfect!' I babbled to Bianca all through break, 'And I love Clara's massive eyes! What do you think they're made from, crystal, glass or jelly stuff?'

'Don't know. Don't care,' shrugged Bianca, folding her arms.

'Why are you so grumpy?'

'I'm not,' said Bianca, turning away from me, 'I'm just sick of you talking about Clara all day!'

I sighed, bit my lip and then said quietly, 'Well, maybe . . . you don't like me making a new friend. But you could be nicer to her, we're supposed to be kind to them. And you have to admit it she is pretty cool.'

Bianca got up and walked off.

After break I tried not to think about what I'd said and drew pictures of Clara with different hairstyles on my interface all through the history lesson about Transport Through the Ages. I only stopped when Louis whispered, 'Yo, Pie Face, how is that a diagram of a jet plane!'

Bianca and I sat next to each other at lunch but we hardly spoke, so eventually I said, 'I'm sorry I talk about Clara all the time. But it's exciting, isn't it?'

'Not really,' said Bianca, fishing strands of noodles out of her pot with her fingers.

'How about we have a sleepover at mine with Clara? You and me, at my house?'

Bianca looked at me, 'A sleepover with a robot girl, that's not going to be fun.'

'Well even if it's not going to be fun, exactly, it will be an historic event! We can be the first people in the world to have a cyborg sleepover. You and me! One day kids will be studying us in history! Bianca and Lyla The Cyborg Sleepover Pioneers!'

Bianca sighed, 'Maybe, Bug Eyes . . . maybe.'

CHAPTER FIVE

On Wednesday morning I did my hair extra nice and neat and wore a whole lot of my Raspberry Sugar Babe Fragrance I got for my birthday.

'You stink!' said Gus in the car on the way to school. 'You totally STINK! MUM SHE'S GIVING ME ALLERGIES!' He did fake coughing all the way there.

When I got to school Bianca raised an eyebrow, 'Ooh Bug Eyes with neat hair! Who are you trying to impress?'

'No one, I just thought . . . since the cyborgs all look so lovely and neat I'd make an effort.'

Louis appeared above us on his flyke. He did that

annoying thing people do on flykes—pedalling down fast like they're going to crash onto your head then breaking and zooming back up a bit. 'Made you jump!' he shouted down to us. 'It's cyber kid day again! Jaspy's on his way!' Then he zoomed off round the corner to land his flyke in the shed.

James and Mercedes arrived and stood next to me and Bianca. We all watched Louis wander back from the flyke shed, his coat just on his head, hanging from the hood, his Edu Hub bag held upside down.

'What a loser,' muttered Mercedes. She narrowed her eyes as she watched him walk towards us. 'How did he get a cyborg? And he gets the cutest one! So not fair!'

· ✳ ⭐ ✳ *

Mr Caldwell let us into the coatpod.

'I bet that Jasper is relieved he got me instead of you two!' said Louis, shoving his coat into the suction hatch. 'Got him a present! To make little Jasper feel even more welcome! Don't expect cyborg kids ever get a present. Little Jaspy's gonna be pretty pleased with this!'

'What is it?' James said.

'One of my old baby toys, a little flying moonshuttle thing, plays a tune, bit bashed up, but Jaspy'll love it.'

'Jasper's eleven!' said James. 'He's a genius! He speaks like a thousand languages! He won't want your old baby junk.'

Louis looked hurt and stomped off into the classroom, 'Well at least I'm making an effort with little Jaspy! Not like you James. You just ignore yours!'

But Jasper liked his baby toy. All morning he sat on Louis' desk holding it close to his face like it was a puppy and kissing it! He kept saying to Louis over and over, 'Thank you, Louis! This is the best day of my life!'

'Thank you, Louis! This is the best day of my life!'

'Thank you, Louis! This is the best day of my life!'

And Louis had to keep whispering over and over, 'No worries, mate.'

'No worries, mate.'

'No worries, mate.'

So in the end Mr Caldwell said it was a great present from Louis and Louis was very kind but it might be an idea if Jasper just put the baby toy on the maths helmet shelf till the end of the day.

'I'm gonna get Clara a present, too!' I said to Bianca while we washed our hands in the persovaps before lunch.

'Well they're obviously easily pleased!' she said, then she sighed and said, 'Do we have to hang out with her this lunch break?'

'Bianca, I'm in charge of her, I have to be with her. It's my job to like her!'

'OK,' said Bianca, glumly, 'I'll come.'

· ✳ ⭐ · ✳ *

That lunch break the three of us sat on the wall again, Clara between me and Bianca like before, 'How do you find Lime Grove Edu Hub, then?' asked Bianca.

Clara turned to look straight at Bianca, 'Lime Grove Edu Hub is located in the Outer Eastern Zone of Landmass Eleven!'

'That's right,' said Bianca. 'But do you like it?'

'Yes, I like it. I like it because Lyla is here. Lyla looks even more lovely today! She smells of fresh fruit today!'

'We've all noticed,' laughed Bianca.

'Yes we have all noticed,' said Clara seriously. 'And we are all so happy to see and smell beautiful smelly Lyla!'

'Anyway, Clara,' I said quickly, 'do you, um, have any . . . hobbies?' Trying to change the subject from my beautiful smelliness.

'Oh yes, Lyla! I'm designed to help humankind!' said Clara. 'I'm fully guaranteed for one hundred years!'

'Right,' said Bianca, looking bored.

I stood up and took charge of the situation, 'Shall we

give you a tour of the playground?'

Clara 2.2 jumped to her feet and clapped her smooth hands, 'Oh Lyla, what a great idea!'

'It's just the playground, it's not that exciting,' sighed Bianca, looking down at her shoes.

I turned round and gave Bianca a look, 'Are you coming with us?' I asked.

She got up reluctantly and said, 'OK, beautiful smelly Lyla. I'll come.'

Clara linked her arm through mine and smiled at me, 'Everything is exciting with beautiful smelly Lyla!'

We walked past James who was trying to explain football to Felix Tranquility X. But Felix Tranquility X was saying, 'A game like that could lead to conflict, James! Let's join these peace loving girls as they tour the Edu Hub grounds. Won't that be FUN!'

James silently shook his head, 'NO!', at me while sticking out his tongue and flaring his nostrils without Felix seeing.

So they trailed round with us.

Far away on the edge of the playground we could see Louis and Jasper Microrange Express. Burak and Charlie B were close by, Burak waving his hands about exasperated, 'Just ONE turn with him, Louis? Jasper isn't just YOURS!'

And Louis was saying, 'Jasper has bonded with ME. He needs stability. Don't you know anything about cyborgs? Go on, Jaspy! Run again!'

'Wow,' said James, looking towards them. 'Look how fast Louis is making that thing run!'

Louis was timing how fast Jasper could run round

the playground, we could hear him yelling, 'Forty miles per hour! Go my little man!' Burak and Charlie B kept having to leap out of the way as tiny Jasper zoomed by.

It looked like a lot of fun.

'Can you run that fast?' I asked Clara.

'No,' then she spoke like an advert, 'Jasper Microrange Express is a wonderful compact product, he is the future in an overcrowded universe!'

I continued with the tour, 'So our Edu Hub was first built in 2035, which is why some of it looks so old and grubby. Here is our Low Gravity Centre that we had built after we did a lot of cake sales and stuff.' I was boring myself but Clara 2.2 kept saying, 'Really?!' and 'How can you remember all these facts, Lyla, when you only have a basic human brain?'

'Very basic,' said Bianca, giggling. 'We're all very basic here at Lime Grove.'

I carried on, 'Here are the degraders for all waste!'

And James said all sarcastically, 'The degraders! Wow! And this one says it can process up to one point seventy cubic metres of waste in one hour! And is the property of Eastern Zone County Council! What will wonderful but basic Lyla show us next? Maybe our new friends would like to inspect fascinating playground drain covers, Lyla?'

'Drain covers?!' said Clara, clapping her hands and doing a little jump.

'Drain covers? Yes, please!' said Felix Tranquility X, looking amazed.

'Go on, Lyla!' said James, trying not to laugh. 'Show us the drain covers!'

We all stood round a drain cover in the main playground. What can you say about a drain cover? Not much. Just, 'That's where the rain goes.'

But Clara 2.2 opened her eyes wide and placed her cool smooth hand on mine, 'Really!? It this true, Lyla? The rain drains away! That must mean the playground can stay relatively water free even in a heavy rain shower. Lyla you know so much! Isn't she great everyone?!'

I nudged her hand away and said quietly, 'Honestly, Clara, I hardly know anything. I'm just basic like everyone else!'

Felix Tranquility X placed his arm round James' shoulder in a friendly way and smiled, 'Hey, Clara, you know who isn't basic in any way . . .? This guy here! James Defries! Look at him! Mr Cool! This guy is something else!'

James just stood there making a silly face.

'Well, I'm happy I'm with this super girl, Lyla!' laughed Clara and looked right at me, 'My Lyla is amazing!'

Bianca and James were now doing that silent giggling at each other, making stupid little snorting noises and then pretending it's a cough.

I ignored them and said to Clara, 'Yes, well, as I was saying drain covers help the playground stay water free,' and I nodded slowly, like a professor.

· ✳·⭐·✳ ·

We all walked on. Now I was actually enjoying myself, looking for more interesting features to be all brilliant about. I ignored James who wasn't helping my tour by suggesting stupid things under his breath like, 'Let's go and look at some soil.'

Next I announced, 'Now, here by the Assembly Pod is Mr Martinelli! A robot, like you, only not like you. He's very, very old. He is currently on playground duty. Hello, Mr Martinelli! Here are the new cyborg children.'

Mr Martinelli doesn't have 'Hello' in his vocabulary any more so he just flickered his little green light a bit and said, 'Yes.'

Clara assessed him with a long up and down stare, then said, 'A low-functioning basic robot. Obsolete.'

Mr Martinelli wasn't bothered, he turned his metal can head round and realised there was a micro cyborg getting up to dangerous speeds in the playground, so he trundled away to tell off Louis. I placed my hand on Clara 2.2's arm like she kept doing to me and I said, 'Oh my gosh, yes! Mr Martinelli is nothing like you, he is just an old electrical appliance! Probably more stupid than a calculator!' And I laughed.

'So funny! Lyla! Ha ha!' said Clara.

But after, while we were shoving our coats into the suction hatches Bianca frowned at me, 'Why are you sucking up to the robot kids so much? You're practically turning into one!'

'I'm not! I'm just being nice, Louis is right, we need to be friendly!'

'But they're so... fake! They're not real. Clara's not a friend, Lyla. Listen to her!' she put on a silly robotty voice, '"We are all so happy to see and smell beautiful smelly Lyla!" Who talks like that?'

James shoved past us on his way into the classroom, 'That Felixbot is doing my head in! He's so phony!'

'He's nice!' I said, a bit angrily.

James didn't answer.

When Louis finally came back through the cloakroom portal he was carrying Jasper high up on his shoulders, Jasper was chatting in his high-pitched voice, 'Were you amazed, Louis?'

'You bet! Until old Mr Junky Smelly put an end to it I thought you might get up to supersonic speeds!'

'Oh, I can!' said Jasper, 'Mach 1, no problem!'

'Show me on Friday, when old Junky's not about!'

Louis put Jasper down on the floor gently and then crouched down so he was more on Jasper's level, 'It's PE next, we're doing races! You're gonna love it!' He gave Jasper a little high five and Jasper turned and ran into the classroom laughing his sweet, high-pitched little laugh.

'Yours seems happy!' I said.

'Make an effort with them, Pie Face! You can't just wander about the playground like a bunch of grannies looking at the degraders and drains!'

He rolled his eyes at all of us — Bianca, James and me — and shook his head, 'You're useless!' He waved his hand towards the cyborgs, who were already sitting silently in the classroom, 'They need stimulation, fun, encouragement! I looked all this stuff up yesterday, it wasn't even my homework, and it's a fact, if we treat them nice and really care for them they get better and better!'

'Louis MacAvoy, the new world expert on cyborg development!' muttered James as we all traipsed after him into class.

I looked at Louis chatting to little Jasper sitting on his desk, they both looked so happy.

CHAPTER SIX

'Mr Caldwell! Are you really going to make us race against one another? Friend against friend?' said Felix Tranquility X as we lined up for PE. 'Imagine the emotional pain this will cause? Making enemies of classmates. Stirring up feelings of unbearable jealousy in the losers.'

James said, 'It's only races, we usually get over it.'

And Mr Caldwell said, 'Er, well, we could do . . . dance?' About ten of the boys and Mercedes all started complaining so loudly Mr Caldwell had to blow his whistle to shut everyone up. 'OK! That's quite enough! We will have a session in our Low Gravity Centre!'

Everyone went, 'Yessss!'

· ✳ ⭐ ✳ ·

The Low Gravity Centre used to be so shiny and white inside but it's getting a bit shabby with everyone shoving themselves off the walls. Low gravity is my best subject. I'm good at all the stuff we have to do with the tools, it's so we can do engineering on Mars and places when we grow up. Usually we do a lot of floating about and putting nuts and bolts together. I said to Clara, quietly, 'Low gravity is my best subject. Once we all had to work in teams to put little satellite things together. I was project manager.' Clara 2.2 smiled and said, 'You are simply amazing, Lyla!'

But Louis heard us and said, 'Woah! Watch it Pie Face, your head's big enough already!'

· ✳ ⭐ ✳ ·

I didn't get a chance to show Clara my proper low-gravity skills as Mr Caldwell decided it would be free movement, since the cyborg children had never been in a zero gravity situation. Mr Caldwell put on his choice of music so we could all float about to it. Mercedes said,

'No way am I floating about to this granddad tune!' And she sat down on a bench with her arms folded. Of course, once Mr Caldwell had pressed the zero gravity button she just floated up into the big white space like the rest of us. But she did keep her arms folded for a bit while floating. Louis was holding Jasper's tiny hand as they floated together. 'I'll show you something funny!' he said, 'Watch!'

He made a big blob of his own spit and he spat it out so it was floating about all over the place. 'You try, Jaspy! Make a spitball!'

'We don't have any spit,' said
Jasper. 'We do not require it.'

Louis spat out another ball, 'Don't
worry, I'll do another . . . for you!'

Everyone had to float about
trying to keep out of the way of
the floating spitballs.

At first Mr Caldwell didn't notice, he
was busy floating about
near the music controls
trying to find, 'A nice little
piece of Mozart.'

But then the girls
started shouting, 'GROSS!'

And Felicity was squealing saying,
'Eeew!' And everyone got more and more
noisy, dodging the floating spit balls.

James said, 'Dodge my spit ball
should be part of the Olympics!'

Then Ridwan yelled, 'Yeah, let's
make it harder! All make a spit
ball, so there's more to dodge!'

And Mercedes yelled, 'IF ONE OF THOSE GOES ANYWHERE NEAR MY HAIR I'M GONNA THROW UP AND YOU'LL HAVE TO DODGE MY PUKE!'

Which is when Mr Caldwell finally realised what was going on and turned off the low gravity so quickly Felix Tranquility

X said he was seeing double because of the rapid descent.

All the blobs of floating spit splattered onto the floor, one landing on Mr Caldwell's head.

Mr Caldwell let the cyborg children sit on the benches to try and realign their cyborg vision, but the rest of us had to stand there and get a massive telling off. Mr Caldwell wiped his head, 'I cannot believe that this is a Year Six class! I cannot believe the example you are setting to our cyborg visitors! Who started this nonsense?'

'Louis,' said Jasper Microrange Express, 'I can confirm Louis started the spitballing!'

Louis looked sideways at Jasper, a bit hurt, but Jasper looked back at him and added, 'Because Louis is an innovator and a great thinker!'

Louis nodded, 'Mm, probably true!'

'Louis did it to bring joy to all!' said Felix Tranquility X.

'Not to me!' said Mercedes.

'Everyone was having fun! Wonderful funny fun!' said Clara.

'It was the funniest time of our lives!' said Felix. 'Let us laugh!'

The three cyborgs began to laugh together, again more like the sound of bubbling water than human laughter, little Jasper's laugh higher than the others, a sweet tootling sound. Mr Caldwell looked confused and embarrassed, 'Well, I suppose it was . . . fun. Let's not make a habit of it, Year Six!'

'Mr C! Look! I've cut my knee!' wailed Mercedes.

'Looks more like a very small graze to me. I think you'll live,' said Mr Caldwell.

'It still hurts!' said Mercedes sulkily.

Jasper Microrange trotted towards her and said, 'If it hurts my duty is to heal you. Louis, do you wish me to heal Mercedes?'

'Yes,' nodded Louis.

He placed his little hand over her grazed knee, 'Better?'

Mercedes smiled, 'Yeah! Wow! Just like that, look! It's gone. Thanks!'

'That's nothing,' said Jasper, 'my medical powers are infinite.'

Louis looked at Jasper and laughed, almost to himself, 'Got any powers for sorting out my new step-dad?'

Jasper hugged his little arms round Louis' leg and looked up at him, 'I just want you to be happy, Louis.' And Louis patted Jasper's head.

We all went back to the classroom for some more History of the First Moon Settlers.

'See you all on Friday!' said Mr Caldwell as the cyborg children left that afternoon with Sophia System 4002. She turned as she went and smiled at us, 'Our cyborg children and your human children are learning to work and play together really well, Mr Caldwell! We should talk about the possibility of letting some children take them home or on trips.'

'Great!' said Mr Caldwell. 'Discuss it next time?'

'Yes, Friday. Goodbye,' and Sophia System 4002 led them out in their perfect line.

Mr Caldwell nodded towards them as they filed out, 'And that, class, is how you should be walking when I say get into line. Notice no one is chatting at the back, no one is pushing in at the front. Look and learn.'

On Friday the cyborg children returned. Everything was going fine until we had a lesson in the morning making our models of the First Moon Settlers' villages and Louis decided to laser chop some of Jasper's hair off! Mr Caldwell went crazy, 'What have you done, Louis? Jasper Microrange is NOT your property!'

Louis shrugged, 'But Mr C! Me and Jaspy, we both wanted his hair more like mine and doesn't he look cute, sir? A mini me.'

· ✳ ⭐ ✳ ·

Then in the afternoon James got in massive trouble for turning Felix Tranquility X off! And leaving him in the persovaps, just propped up by the hand dryers! Mr Caldwell spent all of geography asking how he thought Felix could learn anything about human life when he was turned off for thirty minutes. Mr Caldwell took the three cyborg children to one side to say how sorry he was about what had happened. While they were over by Mr Caldwell's desk Bianca asked James why he'd done it and he said, 'Felix is so fake I can't stand it. He just tells me I'm amazing and cool all day but won't play football! I needed a break!'

'How did you learn how to turn him off?' said Bianca.

'Oh, I just asked Felix and he said, "Press my nose". Easy!'

Louis said he should be reported for cruelty to cyborgs. And then James said, 'How was it cruel?' And then I got angry with both of them and said, 'Look, I want to take Clara home for a sleepover! For the first cyborg sleepover EVER! Plus I actually like her! You have to do better with yours. Don't go cutting their hair! Don't turn them off! Or they won't let us take them anywhere!'

Louis said he didn't think Jasper would want to come to his anyway with his new dad there. He said his new dad isn't the friendly type and he might affect Jasper's development, 'He's a bit . . . you know, crazy sometimes.' James said he'd honestly rather have Mr Martinelli for a sleepover than Felix Swanktrility Boring. Louis agreed Felix was really too boring to bother with but he might think about taking Jasper on a trip one Saturday.

'If we're allowed to take them out he doesn't need to come to my house, does he? I guess me and him could go to the Aquadome. I bet he swims like a water rocket!'

James laughed, 'He'll cause a tidal surge in the main pool!'

'Awesome!' nodded Louis, looking excited.

I said, 'Well, whatever. I definitely want to take mine home! So come on, guys, try harder!'

James walked back to his space. And I think he said, 'Yes, Sir Bug Eyes!' as he walked away.

· ✳ ⭐ ✳ ·

When Sophia System 4002 came back at the end of the day she had a long chat with Mr Caldwell, then Mr Caldwell turned to the class and said, 'There have been a few mishaps today, not everyone has been super responsible with our cyborg friends, but . . . Sophia still feels confident that we can invite our new friends on playdates and sleepovers from now on. She thinks, despite the small risks, our cyborg friends need to experience all aspects of modern childhood in and . . . out of school.'

'Who has a playdate in Year Six!' whispered Mercedes to Amia.

Louis put up his hand, all excited, 'Mrs Sophia! Can I take Jaspy swimming in the Aquadome?'

'Yes,' nodded Sophia. 'He operates well in water up to depths of four hundred metres and has his own micro swimwear which we can provide.'

Jasper Microrange looked all excited and turned to Louis, 'When? When will we go swimming together, Louis? Soon?'

Louis patted his little head, 'Just as soon as I have the pocket money sorted!'

CHAPTER SEVEN

'I can't wait!' I yelled over to Bianca as we flyked home above the city.

'For what?'

'For my sleepover with Clara! I mean our sleepover with Clara. You'll come, yeah, to help?'

Bianca flyked with no hands, sticking her arms out like wings as we flew lower over the leafy groves, 'But your parents haven't even said yes yet,' she called back over her shoulder.

'I'll persuade them!' I pedalled faster to catch her up and flyke beside her, puffing as I spoke, 'I know you don't like Clara. I know you think she's just fake and annoying...'

Bianca looked ahead at the sunset, 'She is fake. You only like her because she says everything you want her to say. She's probably programmed to do that.' She looked down at the ground below and said quietly, 'And you're too dumb to see it.'

'Look, I know she's not real. You are. And as a real friend ... will you come to the sleepover? Please?'

Bianca looked at me, 'I guess so, if my mum says it's OK. And ... as long as she doesn't stop us playing Ladies of Mars.'

I smiled, 'Yeah, she has to play that with us!'

Bianca flyked on to her home, a shrinking dot against the evening sun and orange clouds.

I just left my flyke where I'd landed and rushed in, 'Looks like we can have them back to our houses!' I shouted as I ran down the hall to find Dad and Gus.

'Who?' said Gus.

I poured a Luna Lime and grabbed a giant grape, 'The cyborgs! Me and Bianca are going to invite Clara 2.2 for a sleepover!' I sat myself up on the counter, 'If it's OK? Is it? Can we, Dad?'

'I'm not sure, it all sounds a bit . . . risky.' He was trying to arrange four more giant grapes in the fruit bowl.

'Honestly, Dad, they are like the goodest kids ever! I told you! They're perfect!'

'And boring,' said Gus, lying his head on the counter. 'I've seen them at school. So boring.'

'Good and boring?' said Dad.

Gus nodded slowly, 'So good. So boring. Apart from the little one – he's cool!'

'Anyway,' I said brightly, 'we can turn her off if she's any trouble. James turned his off today.'

Gus got down from his stool and started to sing a loud song to himself as he walked down the hall, 'ROBOT KIDS! SOOO BORING! SOOO SNORING! THEY POO BATT-ER-IES WITH ELECT-RIC BUMS!'

'Someone else needs an off switch!' said Dad.

'So can we say "yes", Dad? Please!'

'You're sure we can turn her off?' asked Dad, 'Easily?'

'Yes, by pressing her nose. But honestly, we won't need to.'

'Oh, all right,' said Dad.

'YESS!' I ran off to my room to make Clara her present. I spent two whole hours making her a little Clay 'n' Move model. Of her. It was actually better than the one I'd made Bianca!

· ✳ ⭐ ✳ *

The sleepover was all arranged, my parents had to sign a form and two weeks later I was about to have the First Cyborg Sleepover EVER! I decided to wrap up Clara's present in lovely shiny paper and put one of those strawberry smelly bows on it and I'd give it to her at the sleepover.

'ALERT! ALERT! ROBOTS ARE COMING TONIGHT!' shouted Gus, running down the hall on that Saturday morning. 'ROBOT INVASION TONIGHT! PREPARE YOUR LASER DEFENCES!'

'Gus!' said Dad, 'Clara's not a robot, she's almost human. Lyla sees her as a friend. Clara's extremely advanced!'

'And extremely boring,' said Gus, hauling himself up onto a high stool to eat his breakfast. I looked up at him stuffing aquagro Choccy Boom Blast in to his mouth like some degrader unit.

'Well, she needs to have more interesting experiences,' I said, 'like this sleepover. And me and Bianca are going to show Clara all kinds of interesting things tonight and she will have her first sleep away from her factory and learn to be independent.'

'Exactly,' said Dad.

Gus slid down off the stool and wandered off, imitating me as he went, doing a silly know-it-all voice, 'Me and Bianca are going to show them all kinds of interesting things tonight blah bibbidy boo!'

'And you better not embarrass me!' I said to his little back as he wandered off to watch his cartoons.

I spent the rest of the morning trying to choose something cool to wear when Clara arrived. I tried on everything.

Later Gus peered round the portal, 'Uh oh, bomb site!' He stared at all the clothes everywhere then he looked up at me, 'Why are you in a party outfit?'

'I'm not! It's just normal clothes.'

'No! That's what you wore to Aunty Lana's wedding!'

I ignored him and put a little rose clip in my hair and checked my face in the mirror.

· ✳·⭐·✳ *

Bianca came round at three on her flyke, I went out on the launch pad to watch her pedal down.

'Woah! How much stuff have you brought!?' I shouted up at her.

Bianca was puffing as she pedalled down, 'Too much! It was so wobbly flying over with all this hanging off the handle bars!'

'What did you bring?'

'Oh, just stuff she might like to try!' she said, shaking her hair out as she took off her helmet. 'Make-up. Hair stuff. Mood perfume. A Clone Me set I got last year and never really used . . . just stuff I thought would make this weird event a bit more fun.'

I took some of the bags and we walked down into the kitchen and dumped them on the table.

'I see your teleporter's still broken!' laughed Bianca, seeing the collection of oversized fruit on the table.

Dad walked into the kitchen, 'Hi, Bianca! Admiring our large fruit collection? It's OK with stuff in boxes and packets, it's just the fruit that comes through big.' He made himself a chicaccino.

Bianca walked up to the teleporter and started to set the dials for her house, 'Is it OK to send some of my stuff back to my house now, Mr Hastings? I don't think we'll use all this stuff in one night, I've brought waay too much.'

Dad sipped his chicaccino and shook his head, 'I wouldn't risk It, Bianca, it's really doing some crazy stuff,' and he walked out and down the hall, turning back to say, 'Oh and Lyla . . . I've told Gus it's strictly off limits till it's fixed.'

'OK, Dad!'

Bianca looked at me, 'Why are you so dressed up? It's not a party is it? Thought it was just a sleepover!'

'It is,' I said quickly. 'Come on, let's go and get my bedroom ready!'

· ✳·⭐.✳ *

My bedroom isn't that big, I have a foldaway sleeping pod, but for a sleepover we use the Float 'n' Sleeps. I only have two so I'd had to borrow one of Gus's. I switched them on and watched as they floated up into the air.

'She better not pop mine!' said Gus.

'She's perfect so she's not going to!' I said.

'She better not make my Float 'n' Sleep smell of electricity!'

'Electricity doesn't smell!' I said, patting the Float 'n' Sleeps together in a line to look a bit more stylish.

'What do they smell of?' asked Gus.

'Nothing,' I said to him crossly. 'Don't you have some Moon Wars to play or something? Go away!'

He walked off down the corridor then turned round, 'Well you still smell of that raspberry stink!'

'He's so cute!' said Bianca.

She's an only child.

· ✳·⭐.✳ *

A ROBOT GIRL RUINED MY SLEEPOVER

As arranged, at exactly 18:00 hours the portal chimes went and there were Sophia and Clara. The skyvan from the Luna Livewires Corporation was left on hover mode above the launch pad. 'Come in!' said Dad, 'Welcome!'

'Thank you!' smiled Sophia, 'May I present Clara 2.2.'

'Hello!' said Dad, doing a little bow, like Clara was royalty from ancient times. Gus crept up behind Dad and peered out from behind the safety of Dad's legs.

'I will leave this high-value cyborg child in your care for the next fourteen hours,' said Sophia.

Dad did the maths in his head, 'Ah, so collecting her at . . . eight. Bit early for a Sunday!'

'That is the maximum time we can allow, Mr Hastings! Company policy.'

'Well, of course. See you at eight tomorrow!'

Sophia raised her neat eyebrows and looked hard at Dad, 'See you at eight tomorrow, Mr Hastings, and thank you for allowing this sleeping over occasion to take place in your basic human habitat.'

'Well, it was the girls' idea!' he said, pointing to me and Bianca.

'More yours!' whispered Bianca to me.

Sophia turned and went, neat little steps walking out of the front portal.

For a few seconds we all just stood there in the hallway. Clara blinking her big eyes, tilting her head slowly one way then the other.

'Right . . . well, I'll leave you girls to have fun!' said Dad. 'Let go of my legs, Gus!' he shook Gus off. 'Staying with the girls or coming with me?' asked Dad.

'With the girls,' said Gus, quietly, just staring up at Clara.

CHAPTER EIGHT

Clara 2.2 looked around as we walked down the hall to the kitchen and then she smiled at me, 'I have never been in a real human house. Lyla your house is so beautiful! Just like you. You look amazing! What a gorgeous dress!'

'Oh,' I shrugged, 'this is just how I look out of school!'

'ACTUALLY, IT'S NOT!' shouted Gus, 'She's only ever looked like that ONCE in her whole life at Aunty Lana's wedding!'

'Anyway what shall we do first?' I said quickly, giving Gus a little death stare.

'We could do our nails? Try my mood perfume? Make-up?' said Bianca.

Clara frowned at Bianca and said crossly, 'I don't need that! I'm perfect!' then she spun around to look at me, 'Lyla, you are so lovely but we could enhance your natural beauty!'

Gus laughed so hard he had to hold onto Bianca to stay upright. I found myself tossing my hair about and going, 'Well OK! Why not!'

We got out the glitter lip tints and spread the beauty stuff Bianca had brought all over the kitchen counter top. Clara took charge, 'Lovely Lyla will sit here and we will enhance her beauty. Bianca will be the assistant and pass us the items as required.'

'What's my job?' said Gus.

'Be an assistant with me,' said Bianca, patting Gus's head.

Gus shook his head, 'No, thank you. I'm watching cartoons instead!' and he padded off.

· ✳ ⭐ ✳ ·

Clara's plasticky fingers smoothed my skin with make-up and glitter tints. She brushed my hair and coiled strands round her fingers, 'I have heat settings in my hands, so if I turn up the heat in my fingers it's the same as a curling rod!'

She finished and took me to the hall mirror to show me the finished look. I thought I looked pretty amazing but Bianca giggled and said quietly, 'You look like a mum!'

Gus ran back in to see, 'DID YOU MANAGE TO IMPROVE HER?!'

He looked up at my glittery face and curly hair for two seconds and then ran around in a little circle going, 'AND THE ANSWER IS . . . NOOOOOOOOOOO!'

He stopped spinning, 'This is boring. If you need me, I'm in my room!'

Bianca laughed, '"If you need me"! He's so adorable!'

Clara looked hard at Bianca like she couldn't really understand.

'OK!' I said brightly, 'I'm all made up like this, now let's do Bianca, too! Then we can all play . . . Ladies of Mars!'

Bianca started to put on some make-up.

'What is this game Ladies of Mars?' said Clara, tipping her head on one side.

'We made it up,' said Bianca, swooping her hair up into a crazy high ponytail. 'We pretend we live in a really swanky Mars Colony place and we're these trillionaire women who run a platinum mine and we go shopping every day and talk about our fabulous apartments.'

Clara looked at her blankly, so I demonstrated by talking in my Mars Colony accent, 'Yes, and I'm called Belinda Alvor, darling! I'm twenty-two and I have seventeen swimming pools and a micro-elephant as a pet!'

Clara blinked and tipped her head to the other side, like a dog might, thinking. Bianca poured herself a large glass of Luna Lime and sipped a bit through her lip glossy lips, 'Ahh champagne!' she drawled in her pretend Mars Colony  accent. Then she held out her hand to Clara and said, 'Hello there, stranger! My name is Laura Pavonis, the totally fabulous Laura Pavonis!'

Clara frowned, 'No! NO! Your name was Bianca before!' then she spun towards me and pointed at me, her eyes really wide like headlamps on a skycar, 'You were Lyla! You were my best friend! What is true?'

'I'm still Lyla!' I said, 'We're just pretending, like acting?'

Bianca came up to me and said in her Mars Colony accent, 'Belinda, darling! How's that gorgeous new boyfriend of yours?'

But Clara covered her ears and started talking very loudly, 'I DON'T UNDERSTAND! SHE IS LYLA! SHE HAS NO BOYFRIEND! SHE IS TEN! SHE IS LYLA!'

She was shaking all over, 'HELP! HELP! I CAN'T DO THE PRETENDING LIKE ACTING!'

'She's going to explode! Turn her off! Press her nose!' said Bianca.

I jabbed Clara's nose with my finger, her big eyes closed and she stood quite still.

'OK. Now that was freaky!' said Bianca, 'Let's just leave her turned off for the whole night.'

I looked at Clara all quiet and shut down, I shook my head, 'I can't. This is the First Ever Cyborg Sleepover and the cyborg needs to be a part of it.' I turned Clara back on. As she opened her eyes I said in my normal voice, 'It's OK now, Clara, we won't do any more pretending.'

Gus padded back into the kitchen, 'Was there a fight? I heard a lot of yelling.'

Bianca and I shook our heads, Gus went on, 'Does it want to see my room?'

'Oh yes!' said Clara. 'Let me see more of the basic human habitat!'

We all followed Gus up the hall. Clara's eyes scanned Gus's room slowly, looking down at the toys and clothes on the floor and up at the storage hatches full of bits of Moon Wars playsets and half-eaten packets of jellyfish crispies.

'Excessive disorder,' she whispered.

'Said it before . . . I'm not programmed for tidiness!' laughed Gus, slapping his forehead like it was his best joke ever.

Bianca laughed too.

Clara frowned, 'Little boy! Let me help you!'

And before anyone said anything she went around Gus's bedroom tidying everything. *Everything!* I had never seen a room so tidy. She worked so fast, in silence, putting all his Moon Wars playsets back together, matching up every odd sock and she folded his Moon Army print pyjamas into a shape so small it could fit into his hand. Then Clara made a pile of all the old empty packets of jellyfish crispies and stared at them, two bright beams came from her eyes and vaporised them into nothing.

'Cool!' said Gus, 'What else can you do? Can you pull off your own head and carry it under your arm?'

'Gus!' I said, kicking him lightly in the shin, 'Sh!'

'No,' said Clara, 'I have a complex electrical system throughout my body. If my head came off I'd stop working.'

'We're like that too!' said Gus. 'Can you fly?'

'No.'

'Me neither,' said Gus, 'but I've asked for some of those jet socks for my next birthday. You should get some too, on the advert it shows this girl zooming up to touch her ceiling! And she says, "IN JET SOCKS THE SKY'S THE LIMIT!" But Evan, my friend, he already has a pair and he says actually the ceiling is the limit. They're not that amazing. But they're still cool.'

I showed her my room with the three Float 'n' Sleeps, 'This is where we will be sleeping tonight.'

But Clara said, 'I will not sleep. I will stand and watch over you while you sleep.'

From the kitchen Dad called, 'Who wants food?'

Gus led the way back to the kitchen holding Clara's hand.

But Bianca pulled me back, 'OK, that's TOO weird!' she whispered.

'What?'

'Her! Clara! Plastic face! Watching us while we're asleep! I'm not going to sleep with her staring at us all night! You saw what she did with her eyes! What if she zaps us with her death stare while we sleep? I'm going home if you don't turn her off. Sorry, Lyla, this is crazy! She can't play anything. What's the point of her? I'd honestly rather have a sleepover with someone like Louis! She's just tech! Weird Moon Colony tech. She's not even cute like Sparks.'

She collected some of her stuff from my room and started to walk towards the front portal, 'Tell your dad I'm really sorry but I'm too scared to stay!'

'But, Bianca, please stay!' I said.

She was already out on the launch pad putting on her flyke helmet, 'I can't, she's too freaky! You might like to hang out with robots just 'cause they say nice things about you all the time but I'm going. You can have her or me for a sleepover, but not both!'

'But if you go I'm all alone with her!' I said.

Bianca said firmly, 'You wanted a cyborg sleepover, Lyla! No one else did. You said you liked her!' and started to pedal fast up into the air. And then she was too high up to talk to anymore.

'I'll turn her off, Bianca,' I said, too late. 'I want a sleepover with you not her,' I whispered to no one.

I walked slowly back into the house and found the little gift I'd made for Clara in my room, then I went to find the others in the kitchen. Suddenly this sleepover felt like the worst thing I'd ever decided to do. I was a bit scared and sad at the same time.

'You were a long time!' said Gus, 'Where's Bianca?'

'Bianca went home.'

'Why?' asked Dad.

I didn't know what to say. But Clara said slowly, 'Bianca was frightened.'

'How did you know?' I asked, totally spooked.

Clara shrugged, 'Because I know. I know everything.'

You don't know how to play Ladies of Mars, I thought.

Dad said, 'Well anyway . . . who wants noodles?'

He'd bought loads of special sleepover food, caterfilla pies, flying jelly bat sweets, he'd sliced up one of our giant oranges like it was a melon and he'd bought some technicolour noodles! I really wanted to turn Clara off right then but Dad seemed so into his sleepover food I tried to be cheerful and carry on like it was all fine.

'You don't usually let us have these,' I said, looking at the pile of rainbow noodles shimmering with all those crazy colours.

'Well,' he smiled, 'it's a treat! It's not every day we have a cyborg sleepover! I thought Clara would like to try some classic sleepover food.'

'Dad, they don't eat,' I said quietly.

'Thank you, lovely Lyla's dad, but I'm photovoltaic,' said Clara, 'through my skin!'

Dad looked confused.

'She's solar panelled, Dad, like the car!' said Gus, rolling his eyes. 'So more food for us real human children!' He sucked a rainbow noodle into his mouth.

Dad went to check his messages and Clara sat and watched us both as we ate. Gus was doing his usual eating like a degrader, stuffing catterfilla pies in one after the other, talking with his mouth full of everything. He peered up at Clara. 'Why are... *chomp*... your eyes ... *chew*... so big?'

'Gus!' I hissed, 'Stop eating like a degrader! Sorry, Clara! He's only six!'

'We cyborgs are not allowed out of the factory until we are functioning perfectly at ten years old.'

'Oh, I'm allowed out already!' said Gus brightly, 'Since for ages! Since I was a baby, even. Not by myself. But definitely allowed out!'

I didn't eat much. I pushed my plate to one side and handed Clara the gift, 'Well, even if you don't eat you can have a present from me.'

Clara looked down at it, 'Thank you.' Then she put it on the kitchen counter unopened.

'Open it!' said Gus, 'Here, I'll help you!' He peeled off my wrapping quickly and put the little Clay 'n' Move model back in Clara's hand.

Clara looked at it.

'It's you!' I smiled at her. 'I made it.'

Clara walked over to our degraders and dropped it straight in with all the rubbish!

Gus's mouth fell open with shock, 'But Lyla made that for you! It's really good!'

Clara looked straight back at him, 'But it's not perfect like me.'

No one spoke. I bit my lip and patted my curled hair, 'It doesn't matter . . . it didn't take very long to make. I thought you'd like it.'

Clara looked at me calmly and said, 'I don't like it. It doesn't look like me. It's lumpy and ugly.'

'Right,' I said.

'Who needs soppy presents?! Let's all play MOON WARS!' said Gus, jumping off his stool.

'We're not all six years old, Gus,' I said, feeling a bit tired. 'And Clara doesn't like to pretend.'

Gus sighed, 'OK then. Hide-and-seek?'

'OK,' I said reluctantly, 'Hide-and-seek. I'll just go to the persovap.'

Clara followed me and waited right outside the door

while I went. Which was pretty awkward. I came out, she flared her nostrils wide and said, 'I do not like this smell of faeces. I do not excrete. I never make this smell. I am perfect. I do not like this smell you have made, Lyla.'

'Well you better get used to stuff like this because I'm a real human!' I said and brushed past her to go back.

I let Gus explain the rules of hide-and-seek and he added cheerfully to Clara, 'I'll be on your team at first to help you look.'

'Why do we want to play this?' said Clara 2.2.

Gus shrugged, 'Because it's FUN! Come on! Let's close our eyes and count up to one hundred and give Lyla time to hide. Got it?'

'Oh, yes! Let's have FUN!' nodded Clara, shutting her massive eyes slowly, 'One . . . Two . . .'

· ✳ ⭐ ✳ *

I ran down the hall, I hadn't played hide-and-seek for ages. I tried to squeeze into all the places I'd used before, but I must have been smaller last time I'd played it, probably way back when I was in Year Two or something! I used to fit really well inside the dirty clothes hatch, but not this time. I heard Gus shouting, '99 . . .100! Coming ready or not!'

So I rushed into Gus's room and hid behind his big curtains. I stood there, completely still, my nose pressed against the fabric. It could have only been seconds before Clara yanked it back saying, 'You are found. Come out!'

'That was quick!' I said.

I frowned and looked at Gus, 'Did you tell her where to look?'

Gus sighed, 'No. She can see through walls!'

'High-level Doppler RADAR,' smirked Clara, 'installed behind my eyes.'

'Oh!' I said, 'So . . . how about you hide and me and Gus will look for you? We can't see through walls so it might be a bit more interesting!'

Clara clapped her hands, 'Oh, how exciting! Off I go!' She wandered out of Gus's room while Gus and I counted up to a hundred together then Gus ran ahead of me to find her.

'Oh!' I heard him say, 'You didn't try very hard!'

As I walked into my room there was Clara standing still just covering her shut eyes with her hands, like a little kid, saying, 'You can't see me!'

Gus laughed, 'YES WE CAN! It's just YOU CAN'T SEE US! You dimbo!'

'Gus!' I hissed, 'Be nice! She's learning!'

Clara took her hands away from her eyes. I smiled at her and explained, 'You have to hide your whole body? Like I did before, then we can't see you.'

Gus slapped his head still laughing, 'Duh! Anyone knows that!'

Clara stood very straight and looked at us both brightly, 'Oh, ha ha ha, you are funny, little Gus. Now I understand and I will be the best at this game,' and she grabbed Gus's little chubby wrist. 'Gus, is it our turn to hide this time? We will hide our whole bodies, yes? What fun we will have! Lyla will look for us. And this time she won't find us. Ever.'

'That's right,' said Gus encouragingly, still giggling a little to himself.

Grasping Gus she led him out of the room.

I shrugged and I started to count to one hundred.

CHAPTER NINE

'98 . . . 99 . . . 100! COMING READY OR NOT!' and off I
went, round the house first checking Gus's room, behind
the curtain again and under his sleeping pod. Then in
the persovaps and behind the shower screen. And then
I heard the sound of running feet and Gus whispering
somewhere. I heard Gus saying, *'No, no, I don't think
that's a good idea.'* I ran back towards the kitchen. I
definitely heard Gus saying something like, *'Dad said
no, wait, wait, don't yank me!'* but when I got to the
kitchen and checked all the cupboards and inside the
self-ordering fridge there was no one there. I even tried
to open the teleporter but the door was stuck, 'Piece
of junk,' I muttered under my breath. Dad wandered in.

'Dad, did you see them? We're playing hide-and-seek,' I whispered, 'I heard them somewhere near the kitchen.'

'Ooh that would be cheating, Lyla!'

· ✳·⭐.✳ *

I walked on up to Mum's office, 'Lyla, not in here please! I'm rather busy!' she was hunched over her work.

'But, Mum, did they hide in here?' I whispered.

She looked around her little smooth white room with just her desk and interface. She raised her hands, 'Two children hiding in here? I think we'd see them! Go on, off you go.'

'SAY SOMETHING!' I yelled in the hall, 'GIVE ME A CLUE!'

Nothing.

I thought they might have gone outside on the launch pad.

So I went out there. It was already dark. The cars and skybuses hummed up above in the night sky, red tail lights making a line of slow moving red sparkles in a long line above. And above that all the stars. It was a clear cold night, I could see my breath.

I called out into the dark, 'OK! CLARA! GUS! I GIVE
UP! GIVE ME A CLUE! SHOUT OUT SOMETHING!'

Nothing.

I looked down over the railing at the tops of the tall
trees between the houses rustling in the dark below.

'GUSSY! CLARA! SHOUT BACK!'

'Where are they?' I said to myself softly, 'Where?'

I turned round and looked up at the bright crescent
Moon and at all the city lights of the colonies you can
see twinkling on its dark side.

I walked back towards the front portal and went
back inside.

As soon as I walked in I heard the sound of anxious adult
voices from the kitchen.

Mum was on her chatcom in the kitchen. Bianca's
mum had called, the hologram of her face floated
above the kitchen counter and she was crying. Dad
had his arm on Mum's shoulder as Bianca's mum
talked fast, 'I've called the emergenbots! They're going
to transfer him to the Eastern Zone Hospital.' She

sniffed and wiped a drip from her nose with her hand.

'What happened?' I whispered.

'Sh!' said Mum. 'It's about Gus.'

Bianca's mum went on, 'Our teleporter came on, and I was surprised because it was something being sent from your house. Bianca told me you've been having problems with your teleporter. But I opened the door and . . . there he was! With this cyborg thing!'

She held up Clara 2.2 in her hand. Clara was now tiny, like a doll, she was waving and saying, 'Lyla never found us and I understand hide-and-seek! Ha ha ha!' her voice small and squeaky.

I leaned my head on Mum's shoulder, 'Oh . . . no . . . they teleported themselves to Bianca's house in our faulty teleporter!?'

'What about Gus?' said Dad.

Bianca's mum took a deep breath, 'I'm sorry . . . so sorry,' she wiped another tear off her nose, 'he's really not in a good way,' her voice trembled. 'Bianca, bring Gussy here to show them . . . gently.'

Bianca came into the hologram; she was cradling

what looked like a newborn baby.

My mum gave a scream and clutched my hand.

It was Gus! Shrunk by our teleporter. Bianca spoke softly, 'He's breathing OK I think.' She wiped tears off her cheek with one hand, 'But he's so small!'

Then Bianca's mum shook little Clara angrily at us, 'I said these cyborg kids needed more social skills before they let them out! They don't know enough about anything! I said all along! I warned Bianca, I told Mr Caldwell, I told the head teacher!'

She gave tiny Clara another firm shake, 'What do I do with this now?'

Clara was still laughing even though she was being wobbled about, 'Lyla never found us! Lyla never found us! Lyla never found us! We won! What fun! But why am I so small? Have I made you happy, Lyla?'

'TURN IT OFF!' I yelled, 'JUST TURN IT OFF!'

I watched as Bianca pressed Clara's tiny nose hard and said, 'There! Job done!'

· ✳·⭐·✳ *

We went straight to the hospital to see Gus. Mum flew fast, her hands shaking as she changed the gears and swerved up into the Fly Zone. We hardly spoke. I just looked out into the night sky wishing I could go back in time and not let us all play hide-and-seek, or better, go back in time even further and not invite Clara, and me and Bianca would be having a nice normal sleepover and Gus would be home safe and the right size.

'Can they make him big again?' I said quietly.

'Don't know,' said Dad quietly, 'Let's just get there and see what the doctors say.'

The Eastern Zone hospital is the biggest one in our region, hundreds of floors high. If I stand on my sleeping pod I can see the top of it from my bedroom window. We landed on the big launch pad on the top. We took the lift down through the building to find Gus. So many different departments! All listed on the wall of the lift. I tried to stop worrying about Gus by reading all the names out quietly to myself, 'Organ and bone grow zone . . . Anti Bac . . . Synthetics and repair . . . Centenarians . . .'

'Shh, Lyla, shh!' said Mum, because she was so worried.

They had put Gus in a sort of clear box. He was lying in the box curled up, his dinosaur pyjamas had shrunk too so he looked perfect but tiny. Mum and Dad were crying just a tiny bit, silently like grown-ups can, just wiping tears away. I was crying properly, sniffs and loud gulps. I ran towards the little box and pressed my nose against it. 'Gussy!' I whispered. He turned his tiny little head my way; it was the size of an orange!

He looked very sleepy. In a very small, high voice he said, 'Hello, Lyla . . . why are you sad?'

I said quietly, 'Do you hurt?'

He smiled, 'Not anymore. Look how small I am! I can go round in my Moon Wars playset stuff now, can't I?' He paused, like he was still sleepy and closed his eyes then opened them again smiling, 'I'm just like that little cyborg now! Jasper! Maybe I can play with him and Louis MacAvoy now; those guys always have a great time.'

Dad came up and put his hand on my shoulder, 'Hi, little man, you've had quite an adventure. How you feeling?'

Gus looked up at Dad and said very slowly and quietly, 'Dad, I did tell Clara the teleporter was "strictly off limits" but she said we had to hide really, really well to make Lyla happy, to make the best fun for Lyla. Clara said we had to . . . and I was a bit scared of her then so I said it was probably OK.' He shut his eyes. I wiped tears off my face with my palm and I saw my hand was covered in all the make-up Clara had put on me.

Gus opened one eye, 'You've smudged.'

'I don't care about stupid make-up,' I whispered.

A doctor came to talk to us, 'He needs a lot of rest,' she said.

'How's he doing?' said Dad, his face was all pale.

She paused, 'Mr Hastings, teleportation is never recommended for humans and this case is very severe, Gus will be with us for some time.'

'Will he get back to normal size?' asked Mum.

'Well, luckily this isn't a unique case; there are thousands of teleportation accidents around the solar system annually so we do have the technology to help your son. But he is very young and very seriously affected.'

· ✳· ⭐. ✳ ·

Mum said she would stay the night in the hospital with Gus.

Dad and I flew home.

Our house was so still and quiet without Gus. I took the Float 'n' Sleeps down and got in my normal sleeping pod. I lay there in the dark looking up at the ceiling thinking about Gus so small in the massive hospital. And about my cyborg sleepover. And about how it was all my fault. And about how Bianca had been right all along. And how Clara couldn't play Ladies of Mars and was rude about my poo. I got out of my sleeping pod in the dark and tiptoed to the degrader in the kitchen and picked out the little Clay 'n' Move model of Clara from under some big orange peel and crushed it in my fist. I dropped all the little bits back into the degrader.

CHAPTER TEN

The Monday morning after the sleepover I didn't want to go to school, I said I was too tired and sad, but Mum said going would take my mind off Gus. She was going to see him in the hospital, 'Don't look so worried, love! He's doing well, I promise. He's two millimetres bigger now.'

'That's nothing!' I said, pulling on my flyke helmet.

'Do you want a lift to school?' she asked.

I shook my head, walked out of the front portal and pedalled up off the launch pad.

I had just flown over the parkland and was looking out for Bianca, who said she might meet me above the Broadway Grove, when Louis pedalled really fast up to me out of nowhere and flyked right next to me, so close our pedals almost bashed together!

'Hey! Not so close, Louis! You'll knock me off balance!'

'Yeah well, maybe I don't care if I do!' he scowled. 'I heard about what you did! It's all your fault, Lyla!' he said. Now we were directly above Lime Grove, part of the group of kids making their way down on flykes to the Edu Hub and beginning to circle above the playground.

I steadied my flyke, 'What's my fault?' I asked, starting to pedal down towards the playground.

'You know!' he said as he overtook me, and then landed with a big skid by the sheds. He took off his helmet angrily and shoved his flyke away.

I came down more slowly and wheeled my flyke into the racks.

'What do you think I've done?' I said to his back as he walked off.

'NO MORE CYBORGS AT SCHOOL! EVER! THAT'S WHAT YOU'VE DONE!' Louis yelled back at me as he stomped towards the classroom.

Then he stopped and spun round to face me, 'It's not me who let a cyborg go hiding in a broken teleporter!

I've looked after mine. I've been responsible. You should never have been given Clara. Because of you and your stupid sleepover I'm never going to see Jaspy ever again! And I didn't even get to take him swimming like I promised him. I promised him! I saved up! Promised I'd take him to the Aquadome this Saturday. Now they've recalled the lot of them from school visits! It was on the Eastern Zone News this morning!' and he marched on.

Suddenly I was furious, I ran up to catch him and tugged hard at the strap on his bag, making him spin round to face me, 'I DON'T CARE IF YOU NEVER SEE JASPER AGAIN! I DON'T CARE IF I NEVER SEE ANOTHER DUMB PLASTIC KID! CLARA ALMOST GOT MY BROTHER KILLED!'

Mr Martinelli came over, trundling along on his rusty old wheeled feet, he swivelled his big metal can head to look at me and then Louis, croaking, 'OK? What yelling. About?'

'Nothing,' we both said at the same time and walked off to the cloakroom portals.

It was true, the cyborgs weren't coming back into school. Mr Caldwell told us first thing after registration. 'I know it's a disappointment for some of you, but the authorities feel that these cyborg children can't really be trusted to enter mainstream education yet. There were a few problems over the weekend and as a result the Luna Livewires Corporation has recalled all of them to run a few tests.'

'What! Did one explode?!' shouted Amia.

'No, no! Nothing like that,' said Mr Caldwell.

'Lyla let her one hide in a broken old teleporter!' shouted Louis.

'I didn't let her!' I said.

'That's enough, thank you, Louis and Lyla!' Mr

Caldwell paused and looked grave, 'Clara 2.2 was involved in a game of hide-and-seek that went terribly wrong. As a result Lyla's brother, Gus, has been seriously injured.'

Everyone started whispering, 'Oh no!' and 'Oh my gosh!'

Louis just looked straight ahead and whispered to himself, 'Yeah, and I've lost Jasper, my best friend!'

'My brother is real!' I hissed back, angrily.

'And Jasper's REAL to me!' whispered Louis, still looking ahead.

Mr Caldwell pulled a sympathetic face at me, 'Lyla will need your kindness over the next few days.'

Felicity tapped my shoulder and I turned round to see her blowing me a kiss and mouthing, 'So sorry!'

· ✳·⭐·✳ ·

Everyone huddled around me at break asking about the accident and how Gus was. Mercedes said she'd heard people who'd been teleported never really recovered and James said if it's a new teleporter it's fine as a friend of his neighbour got a free holiday by teleporting himself to a top hotel's kitchen in Tokyo. I got up and went to sit in the coatpod till the end of break because I couldn't stand all the stupid chatting.

Bianca came in too, 'Gus will be all right,' she said. 'He's grown two millimetres!'

'That's nothing,' I sighed, 'Anyway . . . sorry.'

'For what?' asked Bianca.

'For everything! For being so stupid about Clara. Thinking she was a friend. Choosing her and not you for the sleepover. You were right all along; she was just tech, programmed to tell me stuff I wanted to hear. But you're my real friend. You call me Bug Eyes.'

Bianca leant her head on my shoulder, 'Couldn't be a Lady of Mars, either.'

'I would have been better off making friends with a calculator,' I sighed.

'Uh huh,' nodded Bianca.

· ✳·⭐.✳ *

It was the end of break, everyone was coming back inside. James came up to me and said, 'Well, I'm glad you had a sleepover and it went wrong! That Felix Smug thing was so full of itself. I never want to see it again!'

Louis barged into our little circle, 'But you lot never liked them to begin with! You never made any effort! You didn't really care about them like I did. Just liked all the nice things they said about you.' He looked straight at me, 'You didn't give Clara anything. You just showed off in front of her going "I'm so brilliant, look at me!"'

I said angrily, 'What do you mean? I invited Clara for a sleepover.'

'And you shrunk her! You broke her!' said Louis, right into my face.

'No! She did it! She broke my brother!'

'It was your job to teach her stuff! About teleporters, about being nice, about being a real child. And anyway your brother will mend!' Louis said, jabbing my chest with his finger, 'But I'll never see Jasper AGAIN! The best friend I ever had. The only person who's asked me about my new dad and all that stuff. He's gone! And it's your fault, Pie Face! You owe me. You can come with me to get him back from the factory place.'

'I'm not going anywhere with YOU! Jasper wasn't yours, you idiot! He belongs to the Luna Livewires development place, back on the Moon. Plus tonight I have to visit MY SICK BROTHER!'

'Guys!' said James, trying to calm us down.

'What about you, James?' said Louis, 'You wanna come with me to try and get Jaspy back, from the Luna Livewires place? On our flykes? After school?'

'We can't flyke to the Moon, mate. Anyway, I might

have running club tonight,' said James.

Louis looked down at his feet, 'He's not on the Moon, I looked all this stuff up, the swanky head office is on the Moon but they make them in a factory right here, cheaper labour costs on Earth.' He turned to Bianca, 'Bianca? Wanna come with me? It's just in the Outer Sector somewhere.'

'I think I have, um . . . ballet,' said Bianca.

'Yeah right. Sure you do. And that's why I like cyborgs. They're not LIARS!'

And he stomped back to his desk.

That evening Mum, Dad and I all went back to the hospital to visit Gus. Mum and Dad had to talk to a very important doctor while I went close to the plastic box to talk to Gus. Despite the two millimetres he didn't actually look any bigger but he could sit up crossed legged and talk in his tiny voice.

'Hello, Lyla! I'm still so small!' he was laughing, 'I really am like that Jasper!'

'You're even smaller than him!' I said.

'What did Louis make him do today? Did he kick more footballs into space?'

'Oh. The cyborgs can't come to school anymore. They all went back to the factory.'

'But why?' said Gus, he tried to stand up in his little box but it wasn't high enough and he bumped his head. 'Ow!' he sat back down, 'But why?'

'Because of what happened on the sleepover, because Clara teleported you!'

Gus shrugged, 'So what? I'm OK. It's just boring in this box with you sitting there looking like this!' He copied my sad face.

'Sorry,' I said.

'I need better visitors! Bring Louis MacAvoy! And get him to bring Jasper!'

'I can't,' I said, 'I told you, they've all gone back to their factory. Plus Louis doesn't like me now. I'll bring Bianca to see you.'

'I see her all the time!' said Gus, lying back down. 'Go on! Get that Micro Jasper to come in with Louis! Please.'

'I told you I can't.'

Gus looked at me through the glass like a disappointed teacher, 'Lyla, no such thing as "can't"!'

I didn't like life without Gus. It wasn't just that it was too quiet, but we were all worried all the time. Mum and Dad went to the hospital loads. And when they weren't in the hospital they had long serious conversations about Gus's prognosis and Acute Teleportation Syndrome. Sometimes I'd go into Gus's room and look at all his Moon Wars playsets and toy cars and I'd pat his big normal six-year-old sized clothes wishing he'd grow bigger.

· ✳ ⭐ ✳ ·

At school Louis was looking sad every day and getting in trouble for drawing little pictures of Jasper in lessons. He didn't talk to anyone, even the little kids he used to show off to. In the breaks he just leaned against the perimeter fence on the far side of the playground. James and Burak would ask, 'Wanna play footy?' but he'd just shake his head 'no'.

He'd sit next to me not doing any work; he'd stopped borrowing my stuff. I'd say, 'Do you need my memory cube or my stylus?' But he'd just look down at a drawing he was doing of Jasper and shake his head.

· ✳ ⭐ ✳ ·

About one week after the cyborgs had been banned from school, it was home time. Bianca really did have ballet that evening so she was rushing off as fast as she could.

Louis was pulling his old coat out of his hatch and as he did a whole lot of junk fell out, bits of wires, old solar cells from broken helperbots and then finally a sort of little unfinished model of a head made out of Clay 'n' Move. Louis sighed and bent down to pick it all up.

'Here, I'll help you,' I said, crouching down to pick up some of the stuff.

'NO! Don't. I don't want you touching my stuff!' he said and kept shoving things into his bag as quick as he could.

'What is it?'

'Nothing. A science project.'

I picked up the little clay head, 'Is this supposed to be . . . Jasper?'

'No!' said Louis, looking up at me, then he took the head from me and said very quietly, 'Sort of, I'm just trying to . . . make another one. A Jasper.'

I looked at him scrabbling about the floor putting the last bits for his homemade Jasper into his scruffy bag. He stood up. He looked lonely and sad, 'He was learning to listen to me, Lyla. I taught him that. No one else listens to me.'

I nodded, 'So, I'll come with you.'

'Where?' he said, going out of the coatpod towards the flyke shed.

'To the factory. Now, on our flykes. To get Jasper back.'

'Why d'you wanna do that? You don't like cyborg kids anymore!'

I shrugged, 'My brother wants to see Jasper and, no offence, but I don't think you're going to be able to make another Jasper with that junk.'

'Really?' Louis smiled, 'All right! Let's go, Pie Face!'

And he ran towards the flyke sheds.

CHAPTER ELEVEN

Louis and I pedalled up above the playground. Louis was in front, his flyke is so old and battered it squeaked as he flew and I noticed it was bent so he was flying all wonky. 'What happened to your flyke?' I yelled to him, 'You're flying lopsided!'

'Oh nothing, my new dad got mad last week and took it out on my flyke!'

'Oh,' I didn't know what to say, I'd never met his new dad. It was awkward. I looked up at the cars above us, the rush-hour traffic in a long line, the cars glinting as they caught the evening sun. Then I said, 'What did Jasper say about your new dad?'

'Nothing much. But he does this great little fast dance

that's really funny when I'm a bit, you know, upset.'

We flew away from the Edu Hub grounds and high above the Central Zone, taking the flyke route round the huge Trading Hub Dome with its bright hologram adverts rising up into the sky. A huge smirking young man's face was drinking from a Luna Lime and winking his huge shimmering eye and saying, 'Luna Lime! The choice of Moonites!'

'Let's bike through his mouth!' shouted Louis, laughing.

'No, come on, we haven't got time,' I said, 'I told my mum I'd be back for six.'

Then we had to brake to let a group of little kids on their tiny trainer flykes pass, they were with an instructor. There was a line of them, all in their cute little puffy jackets and funny helmets on their little tiny flykes with those big fat stabiliser jets.

'Aw, cute,' I said. 'I remember going to The Little Clouds Flyke Club. I kept flying my trainer flyke upside down.'

Louis sighed, 'Who gets sent to baby flyke class?'

'Didn't you?' I said, starting to pedal again as the line of little kids flew on.

'Taught myself,' he said. 'Cheaper.'

We flyked on, now we were over the far outskirts of the Outer Zone. Over places I'd never been to. The smooth elegant houses of the Central Zone with tree-lined groves and the clear domes of the gated communities were far behind us now. Instead we were above strange old

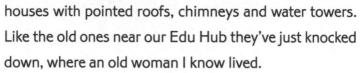

houses with pointed roofs, chimneys and water towers. Like the old ones near our Edu Hub they've just knocked down, where an old woman I know lived.

'Look at the state of this place!' Louis yelled.

I looked down at the ramshackle old houses and dodgy-looking pizza teleporter domes.

'OK, I think we need to fly a bit lower here!' Louis said.

'Do you actually know where this place is?' I asked.

'Kind of.'

'Kind of?' I said.

Louis shrugged, 'Luna Livewires Corporation! It's gonna be a massive factory. We'll see it. Let's go lower!'

We began to pedal down, flyking only a few metres above the ground, looking about for something that might be the Luna Livewires Corporation.

The neighbourhood was so old it had those ancient roads with painted lines up the middle from when they had ground cars. 'It's like our school trip to Yesterday Village!' said Louis.

'Yeah!' I said, 'But with no gift shop!'

· ✳ ⭐ ✳ ·

Louis decided we should land on one of the old pointy roofs to catch our breath and look around. We both held onto an old chimney to keep our balance while we sat on our flykes up on the roof. We looked about.

'There!' I shouted, 'Look! There it is!' I pointed to the far end of a very old street where a massive silver domed building, LUNA LIVEWIRES CORPORATION written in huge letters around it, loomed over the little surrounding houses. We took off from the pointed

roof and flyked towards it, then flyked really low under a silver archway that led into the Luna Livewires Corporation's grounds.

'Look at this massive shiny cyborg factory right out here in this dump, it's hardly the Moon Colonies!' laughed Louis. 'I thought Jasper would come from a much better neighbourhood.' He lay his flyke down on its side by one of the tall curving walls of the dome. We peered up at it.

The bottom of the building was just curved and shiny without any details but further up there were circular windows of different sizes. 'I bet little Jaspy's looking out from one of them waiting for me right now!' said Louis all excited. The dome was set in a small area of trees and flowers, the grass so short and smooth it looked fake. Those expensive little sprinkler bots hovered about showering the plants with water. Outside the front entrance was the skyvan the cyborg children had come to our Edu Hub in with its 'Replica Humans On Board' sign on the back. Then next to

that were some bigger skylorries, the kind that do long distance deliveries to places like the Moon and Mars. They had big photos of Clara 2.2 and Felix Tranquility X on the side and the Livewires logo with 'Delivering excellence throughout the Universe!' written underneath.

The main portal was a huge circular opening, 'LUNA LIVEWIRES CORPORATION – Building better children for a better universe!' shimmering across the entrance. Huge images of Clara and Felix Tranquility X when they were cute little toddlers floated above us with 'Introducing the Clara 2.2 and Felix – turning light into brilliance!' in sparkling lights underneath. For a few seconds we just stood in the entrance looking around at the floating adverts and the smooth, shiny white floor, and then high up at the dome-shaped atrium. 'Look! There's an ad for Jasper!' said Louis, all excited. He pointed up to the right hand side where Jasper's cute little face was a huge moving image turning towards us, waving and speaking, 'I am Jasper Microrange Express, a compact product, the future in an ever overcrowded universe!'

We both stood there looking up, our mouths open.

'Can I help you?'

The atrium was so big we hadn't even noticed a woman sitting behind a desk on the far side, far away. 'Well? What do you want?' Her voice echoed out across the big space.

She peered round her interface as we walked towards her, our footsteps echoing on the shiny floor.

'Well?' she said again as we arrived and stood in front of her smooth desk. She had one of those little hover seats to sit on that are meant to be good for your back and posture. She floated a little closer to have a look at us.

Louis placed his arm on the desk and spoke confidently, 'Just tell Jasper Microrange Express, Louis is here to see him. That's Lou-is Mac-Av-oy, from Lime Grove Edu Hub — he'll know who I am.'

The woman rested her chin on her left hand. I thought she might be a cyborg at first but she had a spot on her forehead so I knew she wasn't. She stared back at Louis, she'd had her nails done with those little moving photos of her pets, so her nails showed tiny spaniel puppies running round and round and wagging their tails. She took a bored intake of breath, 'You want to buy a cyborg child?'

'Not buy him! Just say hello. We're just here visiting,' said Louis, indignant.

'Our cyborg children are worth millions! Do you really think we allow scruffy-looking kids to come in and play with them? I think you better go before I call security!'

Then Louis tried to be clever, 'No, I understand,' he leaned in closer to her face and tried to put on a more grown-up voice. 'The thing is, we are at Lime Grove Edu Hub and we were very lucky to have a few cyborg visitors come to our school and we actually do need to go in and see —'

She interrupted, 'You can't go in and see anybody. I'm calling security! Out!'

She positioned her finger over some little button on her desk, the nail showing a tiny spaniel chasing its tail.

'Wait!' said Louis , 'Wait! I'm actually here because . . . I have to . . . have to . . . to . . . um . . . return a cyborg child!'

I looked at Louis like he'd gone crazy but he stammered on, 'Yes! Because one of the cyborgs that came to our Edu Hub she got lost in the geography resources cupboard and I'm returning her a bit late . . .'

And he pointed at me!

'This is Lyla 3.2, she's an experimental model, a sort of very basic and super-ordinary kind of cyborg. You may not be familiar with her.'

I tried to pull a blank cyborg child face, and I said in a

plain, even voice, 'Hello. How exciting to meet you! I am Lyla Basic Model!'

The woman sighed again, 'Oh please, do I really look that stupid? I'm calling security!'

She pressed the button and immediately Sophia System 4002 arrived, walking fast out of an open portal at the side of the atrium, 'Do we have a problem?'

'Yes,' said the woman with the spaniel nails, 'We do! These dirty organic children won't go!'

'Leave,' said Sophia harshly. 'You must leave. Immediately.'

Louis looked down at his shoes and said very quietly, 'I just need to see Jasper, to see that he's OK.'

Sophia turned towards Louis, 'Request denied. Leave now. Thank you for your compliance.'

Then she began to walk closer towards us, 'Leave!' her voice becoming louder and louder, louder than any human, 'LEAVE! LEAVE!'

'Come on, Louis!' I whispered, covering my ears, 'Before she does something crazy! Like zap us with a laser stare!'

We turned and walked back quickly across the shiny floor towards that huge circular entrance portal, passing the images of the cyborg children in the adverts flickering away.

Behind us we heard Sophia saying, 'Sterilise this area after they have gone. And alert the securobots. Thank you, Louise.'

We heard the *clop clop* of her shoes as she left.

Once outside, Louis leaned against the curved wall and sighed, 'Came all this way for nothing!'

He slid down against the wall and sat on the floor, 'And I'm still puffed from all that flyking!'

I sat on the floor too. I had a carton of Luna Lime left over from lunch so we shared it.

We were just having a little argument about whether Luna Lime was really made on the Moon or actually, like the cyborg kids, made in a factory on Earth that Louis had seen near London, when the huge portal door slid open. We both scrambled to our feet ready for whoever was coming out.

'Look who it is!' whispered Louis, super excited.

Jasper Microrange Express had just walked out of the portal, small and cute as ever!

CHAPTER TWELVE

Louis rushed forward to Jasper, 'Jaspy! I can explain everyth—'

But then another Jasper Microrange Express came out of the portal and stood behind the first. Louis' eyes widened as a third Jasper followed by a fourth and fifth lined up behind the first two.

Soon there were twenty identical Jaspers all lined

up near one of the big skylorries.

'Hey!' shouted Louis, running up and down the line of Jaspers, 'Which one of you remembers me? Louis! Louis MacAvoy?'

All the little Jaspers turned their tiny heads towards Louis and said together, 'Hello, we do not know you! We are a compact product, but we are the future!'

'I can't tell which one is my Jaspy,' said Louis, panicking. He walked up and down the row of Jaspers looking hard at every one.

'Maybe they wiped his memory,' I said, 'and now he can't remember you.'

Before Louis could answer, the huge portal slid open again and we watched as twenty identical Felix Tranquilities and twenty identical Claras all lined up by the skylorry.

'Where are you all going?' asked Louis to a Felix at the back of the line.

'Our group is being exported today to the Moon Colonies as companions for lonely children or to be adopted by childless adults. And I am a Universal Friend Model, meaning I can socialise and bond with absolutely anybody.'

The cyborg kids all walked into the skylorry, the jets fired up and Louis and I stood in silence as the skylorry rose above the clouds.

'So weird to see them all the same together,' I said. 'Come on, we need to get out of here. It's getting late.'

Louis sat on the floor again, but this time hunched up in a ball. He looked up at the sky with his folded arms on his knees, 'What if they've sent my little Jaspy up there and he's adopted by really mean people, what if he has to be friends with a bully who shoves him in a box . . .' and his voice trailed off.

'Louis,' I said, 'we have to go, they'll arrest us or something!'

Louis hid his face in his arms so his voice was muffled, 'What if I never see him again? How will he cope without me? He'll be wondering why I never said goodbye properly. That's the worst feeling ever. Like for me, when my real dad went.'

I crouched down next to him, 'But, Louis, Jasper's not a real person. He's more like a calculator or a fridge. You saw that lot, all the same, like dolls from a factory.'

'I just feel bad,' Louis said, lifting his face up and wiping snot away across his cheek. 'When someone just leaves you and you don't know why, it's hard, probably even for little Jaspy!'

'Honestly, Louis, he won't mind you never said goodbye. He was just tech.'

Louis suddenly got up and grabbed his flyke angrily and started to wheel it round the side of the curved building, 'Jasper is not "just tech"!' he shouted as he walked away. 'And I'm gonna get him back, even if I have to break in to this stupid dome!' And he kicked the wall.

'What about the securobots?' I said, picking up my flyke and catching him up.

'I don't care! I've come this far and I want answers! I want to know where he is!'

Then he stopped walking, looked down at the ground and went, 'Yuck!'

I looked down and there was a human eyeball looking up at us!

'S'not real,' I said, bending down and picking it up. 'Look, it's just a fake one,' I held it up to my own.

'Must be a cyborg spare part!' said Louis.

'Can I keep it for Gus? I want to show him in hospital, he'll love it!' I said and put it in my pocket.

Louis had walked on a bit, 'Look! We can get one for everyone back at school! There's a whole pile of them!' I pushed my flyke on round the curved wall of the dome to catch him up. We were at the back of the building where there were no manicured fake-looking lawns and sprinkler bots, just a big space of waste ground with huge metal containers of junk.

'Woah! That's one big pile of fake eyeballs!' I said, 'And look at all the old circuit boards and wires in that container thing!'

We stood still and looked around. On the far side there was an even bigger container. Along the side it said 'Luna Livewires Corporation – recyclable waste.'

My heart stopped, 'Oh. What's that!? A dead body! Look!'

Poking out from the top of the huge container was a human arm.

'Don't be stupid, Pie Face,' said Louis. 'It's going to be a fake one from an old cyborg!' He plonked his flyke on its side and ran over to the container. He's the kind of boy who can climb up stuff so he hauled himself up and over the edge of the container quickly and stood inside it above me, waving the fake arm about going, 'Guess what I am! An arms dealer! Ha!'

'Get down!' I said, 'We need to get out of here!' Louis trampled about up there on top of the bits of broken cyborg, 'You should come up here, it's weird!

There's loads of fake hair!' He put a long orange wig on his head and peered down at me, 'How do I look?'

'Beautiful!' I said, 'Now get down!'

Louis carried on messing about, 'Want a free pair of hands, Pie Face?' Then he stopped dead, tugged the wig from his head and said seriously, 'Pie Face! Get up here! Look who I found!'

I scrambled up and into the container and walked, wobbling over all the broken bits of discarded cyborgs, to where Louis stood pointing. There was Jasper Microrange, eyes shut, dirty.

'How d'you know he's yours? They make tons of them!' I said.

'Because that's the haircut I gave him. Just like mine.'

Louis bent down and kneeled by his grubby little cyborg.

'Hello, Jaspy,' he said softly.

'Press his nose!' I whispered. 'See if he still works.'

Jasper hummed with that quiet electrical sound for a bit then opened his little eyes.

'Jaspy?' said Louis, quietly, 'It's me . . . Louis MacAvoy. Remember me?

Jasper seemed to be buffering or something, just blinking and looking up at Louis. Louis stroked Jasper's hair, 'You're a bit of a mess, mate. Do you know who I am?'

Little Jasper opened his eyes wide and nodded his cute, tiny head, 'My best friend. You're my best friend Louis MacAvoy!'

'It is my one!' said Louis, punching the air.

Jasper got up onto his little feet, 'Louis! They threw me away!' he said, puzzled. 'Why? They tried to wipe my memory so they could send me to a new owner on the Moon. But I couldn't forget Louis MacAvoy!' he frowned, 'I tried, but I couldn't. Why was that?'

'Oh, Louis is very memorable!' I said, smiling.

Once Jasper had got to his feet we could see he'd been lying on top of the tiny teleported shrunken Clara. Louis and I bent over her. 'Wow, your teleporter really is malfunctioning!' laughed Louis. 'She's tiny! You gonna see if she still works? Wake her up? Go on, press her nose!'

I pressed her nose, it wasn't that I wanted her back, I didn't, but seeing her there I suddenly felt so angry with her for shoving Gus into the teleporter. I guess I wanted a massive argument with her! I pressed her little nose, 'Get up, Clara, we need to talk! How dare you shrink my little brother! Gus told you the teleporter was off limits.'

She opened her little eyes and looked straight at me, and got to her now tiny feet.

'Did you hear me?' I said, crouching down to be more level with her little head, 'Are you even a bit sorry?'

'I'm a second generation Clara,' she said in her tiny voice. 'The first Claras were very good at maths but I am very good at maths and sport. I speak every Earth language and have two Moon dialects. I believe that friendship is the most valuable currency in the universe!'

'Do you even know who I am?' I said.

'No, but I believe that friendship is the most valuable currency in the universe!' she said.

I switched her off.

'You taking her?' asked Louis.

'No, they've wiped her memory,' I said, 'and I didn't work as hard as you did to be really kind to mine. She was never a friend.'

Louis smiled, holding Jasper's little hand, 'Like I always said, Pie Face – I got the best one!'

Suddenly deafening sirens filled the air, 'INTRUDER ALERT! INTRUDER ALERT!'

We looked over towards the dome where a whole line of ugly-looking securobots were whirring up their little head propellers and rising up to fly towards us.

'COME ON!' I yelled, jumping down from the container. 'Let's get out of here!'

'Help me bring Jasper!' shouted Louis.

I tried to help him lug Jasper over the edge of the container but we dropped him. The securobots had circled about us like huge angry insects still screaming 'INTRUDER ALERT!' over and over.

'We have to go, Louis!' I said, covering my ears.

'I'm not leaving Jaspy!'

'THIS LAND AND ITS CONTENTS ARE THE PROPERTY OF THE LUNA LIVEWIRES CORPORATION!'

'Come on, Louis!' I said, running towards our flykes.

'I won't leave Jaspy!' cried Louis.

'THIS LAND AND ITS CONTENTS ARE THE PROPERTY OF THE LUNA LIVEWIRES CORPORATION!' screamed the securobots.

'You have to!' I yelled. 'He's not yours! We'll be arrested if we take him!'

So we ran, leaving Jasper on the floor just staggering to his little feet. We grabbed our flykes and pedalled like crazy. Behind the terrible noise of the securobots I could just hear Jasper's tiny voice, a little high pitched wail, 'Louis MacAaavoyyyy! Don't leave me here! They'll break me down for spare parts!'

· ✳·⭐·✳ *

As we flyked up I saw Louis was really crying now, looking small and defeated as he pedalled his slanting flyke. He wasn't even looking where he was going, just looking down at the roads and old houses below. Tears dripped off the end of his nose. He gulped back his tears, still looking down at the ground, 'You don't understand, Pie Face, 'cause you've got Bianca and a brother and a nice flyke and normal parents . . .' but then he suddenly stopped, threw his head back and laughed and shouted out, 'Yess! That's my little man! Look at him go! LOOK DOWN THERE, PIE FACE!'

· ✳·⭐·✳ *

Far below, Jasper Microrange Express was running at his amazing speed through the streets, following our route in the air. 'He's followed us!' said Louis, delighted. 'Now that's a devoted electrical appliance!' He yelled down to Jasper, 'I'll flyke down and pick you up, Jaspy! Wait there!'

We flew our flykes down to meet Jasper. Louis hugged him and put him gently sitting on the handlebars, 'Hold on tight, Jaspy!'

'But . . . is this stealing?' I said nervously.

'Nah,' said Louis, 'I think if the product follows you out of the factory it can't be. Jasper's stealing himself.'

It started to rain as we flyked home. So we pedalled up higher just enough to be above the clouds and stay dry.

Louis turned off at the Trading Hub Dome, 'We go home this way,' he said, patting Jasper's head. 'See you on Monday, Pie Face!'

'Hey, Louis!' I said, 'It's Saturday tomorrow, doing anything?'

'Probably training little Jaspy, why?'

'Wanna visit Gus? In hospital? He asked for you, you and Jasper.'

'Yeah. OK, we'll come,' said Louis. 'You'd like that, wouldn't you mate?' Louis ruffled Jasper's hair and Jasper smiled up at Louis, 'Yes, Louis MacAvoy.'

I flyked on, above the grey clouds, then dipped under them to reach my house.

When Louis and Jasper walked in to Gus's hospital room that Saturday Gus was so excited he yelped, 'WOW!' and then stood up too fast and banged his head on his plastic box again, 'Ow!'

'I did it!' I said to him, 'Brought your favourite visitors!'

He squished his tiny face to the plastic side of his box and kissed it, 'I love you, Boggle McScruff Pants!' he said, 'Hello, Louis! Hey! Hello, Jasper Microrange – I'm almost as tall as you!'

Jasper Microrange came closer to Gus's box, 'We are both compact products. We are the future!'

'Yes, but I'm not meant to be compact!' said Gus laughing, 'I need to be bigger!'

Jasper put his small head on one side like he was thinking. 'Acute Teleportation Syndrome?'

'Yes!' I said, 'that's what he's got. How did you know?'

Jasper turned to me and said, 'I am a Jasper Microrange Express!' he looked back at Gus in his box, 'I have the capabilities to cure this,' and placed his small hand on the side of the box while shutting his little eyes, 'Louis would you like me to cure Gus?'

Louis took an important breath in and said regally, 'I would!'

'One minute, Louis MacAvoy,' said Jasper, 'while I cure this child.'

A second later Gus was visibly returning to normal size, 'Oooh this feels itchy!'

I quickly called for the doctor. She immediately opened the box so Gus could continue his growth spurt!

Louis stood back looking smug, 'Jaspy, what a star!'

'Is this compact cyborg yours?' asked the doctor, turning to Louis.

Louis nodded proudly, 'He's mine.'

'You're a very lucky boy,' said the doctor. 'We can't afford even one of these amazing cyborgs for this hospital!'

Jasper looked up at the doctor and said in his sweet, high-pitched voice, 'I over bonded with Louis MacAvoy. I can only take orders from Louis MacAvoy. I'm recyclable waste, doctor. I'm defective.'

'BUT I'M NOT. I'M ALL BETTER!' said Gus, doing a crazy little dance which Jasper copied.

· ✳·⭐·✳ ·

Gus was allowed home the next day. Mum bought him a new Moon Wars playset as a welcome home present and I let him have my Nano Ted for his sleeping pod. That night he put Nano Ted next to that fake eyeball I'd given him on his pillow. He chose caterfilla pizza and ice cream floats in hover cones for lunch. 'How much did you miss me?' he asked, chasing the floating ice cream round the kitchen with his tongue sticking out.

'Lots!' I said.

Two weeks later we got a new teleporter! It was the latest design. Gus said he missed the giant fruit. Dad said he didn't, especially Gus leaving massive banana peel everywhere. Bianca came for a sleepover the weekend it arrived. We all stood round it looking at its modern controls and shiny sides. Gus said, 'These new ones are great! My friend Evan said you can teleport yourself to Florida in these no problem! No shrinking! No nothing!'

'Well, we're not trying that,' said Mum firmly. 'This one is just for food.'

Gus padded off to play with his Moon Wars stuff, 'Come and get me, Bianca, if you want to play hide-and-seek again.'

But we didn't. We played Ladies of Mars. Being Belinda Alvor and Laura Pavonis. We put on glitter lip tints and did our high-up ponytails and pretended the Luna Lime was champagne all over again and discussed all the problems we were having with our new cyborg servants in our massive Mars Colony Houses.

I sipped my 'champagne' and said, 'Oh my total golly gosh, darling, Laura, did I tell you! I got three of those Clara 2.2s!'

'Three! That must have cost you trillions, Belinda!' shrieked Bianca, flipping her ponytail about.

'No, not at all! They were on special offer at Marz Mart. Three for the price of two! I've got two doing my gardening and the other one sorting my designer shoe collection.'

'But, darling, are they reliable?' said Bianca in her drawly Laura Pavonis voice, 'They malfunction all the time. I heard in the salon they can burn through your whole crystal trim knicker collection with just one little laser stare!'

We laughed so much Luna Lime came out of our noses.

The End

A MOON GIRL STOLE my FRIEND

WRITTEN and ILLUSTRATED by
REBECCA PATTERSON

It's 2099. Lyla lives in a world of robocats, flying sweets and instant snow, but some things never change. Little brothers are still annoying, school teachers make you cringe, and, when your best friend deserts you for the new girl, it still HURTS. Especially when that new girl is from the Moon. But Lyla's problems lead her into unexpected adventures . . .

'Superb'
Guardian

'A funny and touching story'
Scotsman

9781783447985